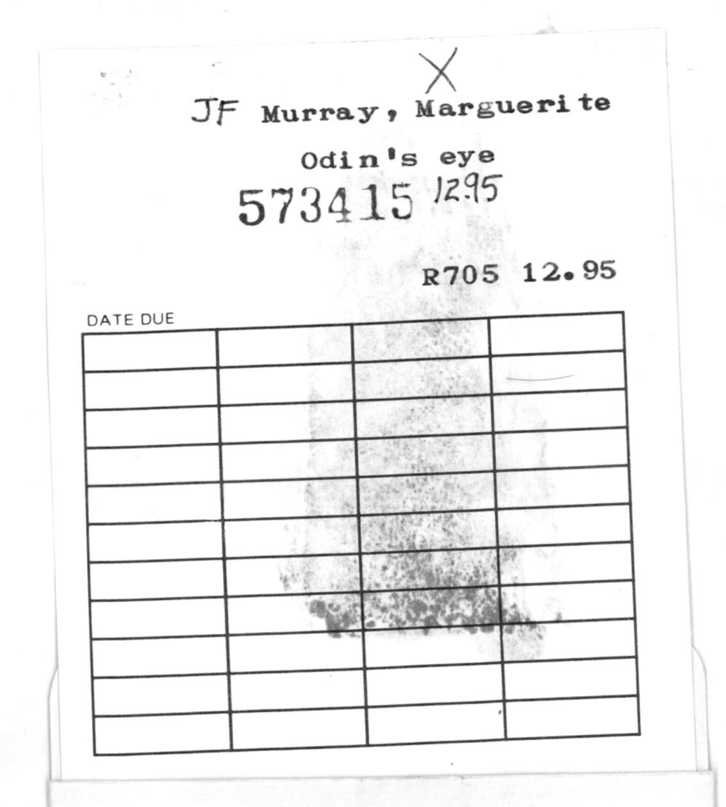
JF Murray, Marguerite
Odin's eye
573415 12.95
R705 12.95
DATE DUE

Odin's Eye

Odin's Eye

by Marguerite Murray

ATHENEUM 1987 NEW YORK

Atheneum
Macmillan Publishing Company
866 Third Avenue, New York, NY 10022

Type set by Haddon Craftsmen, Allentown, Pennsylvania
Printed and bound by Fairfield Graphics, Fairfield, Pennsylvania
Designed by Jean Krulis
First Edition

10 9 8 7 6 5 4 3 2 1

Library of Congress Cataloging in Publication Data

Murray, Marguerite. Odin's Eye.

SUMMARY: Fifteen-year-old Cicely's summer job at a seaside boarding house owned by a relative turns into a dangerous adventure as she stumbles across clues to a long unsolved murder and possible espionage.
[1. Mystery and detective stories. 2. Spies—Fiction] I. Title.
PZ7.M9630d 1987 [Fic] 86-14118
ISBN 0-689-31315-2

To our grandchildren

and To

Evelyn Wainwright Turpin,

who kindly "lent" me

Odin's Eye.

ODIN'S
EYE

ONE

If I had known that Mother had murder on her mind . . .

"*Why* did you call me 'Cicely?' " I had just asked in despair. I was sitting on the kitchen stool, a mistake. You can't be impressive from the top of a stool, and the effect I had hoped for was not working. "Did you *have* to pick 'Cicely' out of all the million names in the world? It sounds like a pot of herbs in somebody's cottage window." My mother looked up from the sink where she was washing beans and frowned slightly, a good sign. I readied myself for an argument.

"The way you say it, it sounds more like the opening chord of one of those dismal things you thump out on the piano," she commented. "What's wrong with 'Cicely?' You could have been called 'Olive Plumtree,' or something like that. Olive was in my homeroom in high school, and she hasn't been heard of since."

I should have known. It was hopeless. My mother is incapable of logical argument. We were now headed down a road neither of us intended to take, a byway. Who *cared* what became of 'Olive Plumtree?'

"My knees are put on lopsided," I said, trying again.

"Well, what do you expect me to do about it at this late date?" Mom asked, sensible, merciless. "Here, string these." She handed me the colander of wet beans and opened the refrigerator, to study its insides. Wet beans are a meager consolation for any problem, and I decapitated three of them and laid them out on the table in front of me. Then I lined up their pointy heads with a space between to show where they had been guillotined.

"Cicely!" Mom said, exasperated. "Get on with it!" She plopped a meat slab onto a plate of flour, laid it out on the counter and attacked it with a cleaver. Whack! Whack! Whack! White clouds rose to her elbows, and the meat lay mutilated before her.

"What on *earth* is the matter with your knees?" Mom asked patiently, as of a child.

My knees are at least three-quarters of an inch off center, that's what. In almost fifteen years of life with Mother, you'd think she might have noticed. I looked with disfavor at my middle-aged-shaped parent—I'm afraid I'm doomed to have her figure. But of course she hadn't noticed. She was already into worrying about her grandchild, Georgie, and from time to time, Winnie, my sister, and her husband, John, my brother-in-law, and even occasionally, my older brother, Newton, who is off and away. I, the late late child, am expected to fend for myself.

"When I walk down the street in my cutoffs, I can hear every boy for miles around saying, 'Here comes Cicely Barrows, whose knees are put on backwards.' "

"Nonsense!" Mom said. She jabbed the meat with a fork and dropped it into a red-hot frying pan. Black smoke dimmed her from view, and sizzlings and cracklings drowned out any attempt at debate. She flipped the meat over, we went through smoke and flame a second time, and then she drenched everything with water from the teakettle. There followed a fearful bubbling and uproar, quenched at last by Mom's slamming a lid on the skillet.

"No boy is going to worry about your knees, Cicely!" continued my mother, as calmly as if murder and carnage with the meat had not just been committed right before our eyes. "But you scare everyone off. Do you have to be so—prickly? Do you *have* to argue with every last boy that comes along?"

"Well, if they say dumb things, I do," I said. The boys around here are really stupid, and none of them like me very much, except maybe Albert Custis. He's the only one with any brains, and he's into Russian ballet. He does pliés in the backyard behind the garage —he told me he does—but sometimes I wonder if he remembers that I even exist. I might just as well be a microphone on a stand. He talks *into* me and then waits for me to play everything right back so he can hear all the beautiful things he said about Nijinsky.

After I'd gone to the library to find out who Nijinsky was, I tried out some of Bertie's points on Mother, but I didn't make much headway. "That Bertie!" she moaned. She doesn't like him any better than I do, but she thinks he's my last and only hope.

"Cicely," Mom said gravely, "you scare the boys to death. Most of the time you talk just like a book."

"Which one?" I asked, a perfectly logical question.

"I don't know," she answered impatiently. "The last one you've read, I suppose."

Kristin Lavransdatter, I thought. I talk just like *Kristin Lavransdatter.* I'd gotten tired of walking back and forth to the library, and I'd taken home the biggest book I could find. And of course I became really interested in all poor Kristin's hardships. Just the same, it was a depressing thought.

"I don't see how you can help the way you talk if that's the way you think," I moaned. "If people don't like to read, obviously they aren't going to like *me.*"

"Well, you don't have to impress every boy with your intellectual genius," Mother suggested.

"I'm not an intellectual genius!" I shouted. I banged the colander on the table, and the top beans jumped out in panic. "I can't pretend I'm a dumbell, that's all."

"You sound just like Olive Plumtree—she used to go on like that," my mother mused. "Come to think of it, I can't imagine why I am thinking about it." Then she appended one of those stray thoughts that always buzz around her. "She was Croatian."

I ignored this, as I usually do these small, mosquito-like irritations of hers, often to my later sorrow. Mom looked thoughtfully at a row of small utensils hanging from hooks on the wall, and selected a potato peeler. "I wonder what happened to Olive," she said. "I don't suppose she ever got married."

"Well, bully for Olive Plumtree!" I yelled. Mother laid the potato peeler down and put one hand on the table, the other on her hip. She looked straight at me, and I took a mental step backwards. Mother is patient —to a point—but even if her hair is currently fading, it was red once and her temper matches it.

"You don't need to yell," Mother said, her own voice rising to a pitch. "If you're going to have any boyfriends at all—and I assume you would like to have them, otherwise why all this Sturm and Drang about your knees—you've got to show a little interest."

"And the minute you do, you find yourself married and down scrubbing on your marrowbone! At least that's what you always say happened to you," I spit back. This was a reckless remark—honest, but in terms of future consequences, reckless.

"Cicely . . ." said Mother ominously.

"You could have been doing something interesting in your life," I observed. "Like dear cousin Millicent that you're always talking about. I bet she doesn't spend her life whacking furiously at round steaks."

"Furiously?" repeated Mother, even more ominously.

"Underneath, you were probably furious at Pop," I explained, eyeing my parent a little nervously.

"Cicely Barrows!" Mother shouted, "I was pounding flour into a round steak for dinner. I was not beating the daylights out of your father! For your information, I am perfectly content with my life!" The red in her hair seemed to grow brighter. But I was getting mad, too, even if my hair is dark like my father's, what remains of it, and I am a beautiful little feminine edition of him, Mother says.

"If you're so content with your life, then why are you always telling me about Millicent's?" I shouted back.

"Millicent," said Mother in lethal tones, "was once engaged to a man named Lummie, and he broke it off. She picked up her life all right, but she's never found anyone else."

"From what you've told me about her, she's probably too smart for most men," I observed.

"Probably," said Mother with a pleased look, and I saw that I had fallen into a trap. "Millicent was very envious indeed when your father came along and carried me off."

It took some imagination to work through this last sentence, since what my mother has gained in stature over the years, my father has lost, and I was mulling when Mother said, "Strange, though, that you should mention Millicent."

I was instantly alert.

"She's invited you to stay with her this summer," Mother said. My anger suddenly evaporated. "At first I thought not," she added slowly.

"Why?" I asked, curious.

"Well, her way of doing things is different from ours," Mother said reflectively. "Though that's not what was worrying me."

"Well, what was, then?" I asked patiently. "I assume

I'm going." You have to allow parents time to work through all the layers of their lives.

"Millicent inherited one of those spooky Charles Addams type places from her grandfather. It's on a remote New England shore somewhere. In the summertime she runs sort of a vacation home for a few of her friends. They're inclined to be intellectuals, you know." I didn't know, but all I could do was wait and hope that my fate was not hinging on my I.Q. or that of Millicent's friends.

"Apparently she needs someone to give her a hand with the housekeeping. You could handle that part all right, Cicely. I don't believe it would be too demanding. She's bought a dishwasher . . ."

"Saved," I interjected.

"I've decided you ought to try it," Mom said reflectively. "She's going to pay you, and you haven't anything else to do this summer. If you *want* to go, that is. Winnie and John think it's okay." I saw that I had been discussed. "Probably you'll be right at home with her friends," Mother continued, "and then again, it might open your eyes some. Being with a houseful of Millicent and her friends."

"They sound positively terrifying," I observed. "But something tells me that there's worse to come."

"Well, you see, this drone Lummie will be there," Mother said darkly. "Millicent's kept in touch with him over the years, but I never thought he'd actually turn up."

"And now she's shacked up with him!" I exclaimed.

Mom gave me one of her shut-up looks. "At fifty-five?" she asked. "Certainly not."

Losing all patience, I yelled, "What *is* the problem then?"

"Cicely!" yelled Mother in return. "I'm trying to *tell* you! There was a murder."

"Oh," I said.

At this point, the kitchen door rattled, and John, Winnie, and Georgie in arms entered and made straight for the skillet. John lifted the lid.

"Oh boy," he said, "are we invited for dinner?"

"If Cicely ever gets those beans strung, you are," replied my parent. I set hastily to work. "I was just talking about Millicent," she added.

"I've discovered that there was a murder," I said. "At long last. But it wasn't Lummie. He's turned up."

"He's come back to the scene of the crime," announced Winnie. "I bet anything."

"*Who was killed?*" I hollered.

"Look Cicely," Mother said patiently. "Millicent lived with her paternal grandfather all during her childhood, in this big old house by the sea. When her father was killed in the war, Millicent and her mother simply stayed on with the grandfather. I don't think she was very happy, and she left home when she was sixteen. Her grandfather, who ended up a cripple, died suddenly, maybe twenty-five years ago, and the very next day, his close friend, a Peter Kugle, was discovered shot to death. I don't know the details, but this Lummie was fighting with the grandfather when he died, and though he was not implicated in the friend's death, *something* happened, because that's when he broke off the engagement to Millicent and simply walked out of her life. That's all I've ever been told."

"It seems almost enough to have been told," I observed. "Or perhaps a little more than enough." Winnie laughed and dug into the bean pile. "I'll help," she said. Georgie, in her lap, was already helping.

"I don't like unsolved murders," Mother stated in a worried tone. "Skeletons fall out of closets."

"Surely you can trust me," I said, and Winnie's laugh caroled through the kitchen again.

"Oh, sure," said Mom, with a certain amount of sarcasm. Then she continued reflectively, "I've really been of two minds, Cicely, but I guess . . ."

"You *are* going to let her go then." John's statement didn't leave a whole lot of room to move around in, and Mother looked sort of startled. I like my brother-in-law. He's a big, tall guy with lots of black hair and a beard. He doesn't get excited too easily, and he takes a while to settle in his mind what he's going to say. But that doesn't mean he either thinks or moves slowly. He pilots private planes for these big corporations, and he's always got kooky stories about the VIPs he flies around. I wasn't surprised he'd stuck up for me. "How's she going to get there?" he asked.

"Millicent said she'd pick her up in the car. Next week Tuesday, if I agreed," said Mother in a resigned tone.

"Sorry I can't fly you up, Cicely," John said. "Some other time. I'm off that whole week to the West Coast." He sat down on a stool where he could sniff the goings-on in the skillet.

"I'm going to be widow-for-a-week," explained Winnie, removing squeezed beans from Georgie's fist and then squeezing him. "I was counting on Cicely for aid and comfort."

"I'm bound out to Millicent, I perceive," I remarked.

"I love Millicent dearly," said Mother, ignoring all superfluous and intervening comments in the hardened way of parents. "She's perfectly responsible, though I doubt she'll notice your knees are out of orbit, Cicely."

"What knees?" asked Winnie.

"Millicent's always sounded fascinating," I said, in what I hoped was a voice of cheer.

"You know, she's a book review editor or something in New York," Mom continued, "and your father never can think *what* to say to her. I've never been to this creepy-crawly place of hers, but I've heard a lot about it." She frowned and looked sadly at me, as if I were already lost. "I always thought it sounded beastly, sort of rattletrappy and full of mice. And murder . . . and now this Lummie coming back. . . . I don't even like the name of the place. It's called 'Odin's Eye'."

— Two

So there I sat on the front porch, like Rebecca of Sunnybrook Farm, only smarter, surrounded by my bags, and waiting for Millicent to pick me up and take me away for the summer. A nondescript gray car wheeled around the corner and made an elliptical landing, simultaneously biting a chunk out of our front lawn. Millicent got out of the car. I could see that she was a determined woman. She was short and sturdy, I wouldn't quite say chunky, and she looked athletic, or at least as if she were strongly in favor of vigorous exercise. She walked with purposeful strides onto the front porch and skewered me with a look of appraisal.

"You're a living edition of your mother, Cicely," she said.

"Heavens!" I responded, rashly, but from the heart. Millicent's eyes glittered—with humor, I hoped—and her thin, pointed nose twitched, but to my relief, the subject was not pursued.

"Well, Millicent!" said Mother, coming to the door and holding it open. "She's all yours."

"Fine!" said Millicent heartily, and with what I felt was sincerity.

"Jason asked me to tell you how sorry he was to have missed you," Mother said insincerely, in fact, falsely, since Pop had left for the office thirty minutes early in order to avoid the encounter.

"Jason—" said Millicent vaguely. She seemed to have trouble placing him. Maybe all these years she'd thought Jason was the dog.

"Do come in," said Mother warmly, now that Pop was safely dismissed from the conversation. "It's so nice to see you again. I have coffee all ready."

"We can spare exactly twenty minutes, Caroline," said Millicent, consulting her watch. "I have reserved for luncheon at straight-up twelve, and we have a long way to go."

Mom and Pop always creep apologetically into restaurants, and Mother has never reserved for anything at straight-up twelve or any other time. Nevertheless, she nodded knowingly, and we fell upon our crumpets. Mother used up nineteen and one-half minutes of the twenty describing my relationship with Bertie Custis—mothers will dredge up a boyfriend for their daughters if it kills them. At the end of the recital, you'd have thought Bertie had plighted his troth. Millicent gave me one or two scrutinizing glances, catching me off balance because I had become so engrossed in my parent's version of Bertie and me.

Earlier that morning, I had received another nineteen and one-half minutes of Polonius-type advice from

Mother, so our second farewell was short, although, like all travelers setting forth for the unknown, there was a tinge of wistfulness in my good-bye, and Mother continued to stand in the doorway, waving.

With some navigational instruction from me, we at last reached the freeway. Millicent launched the car up the ramp and catapaulted into the traffic without so much as a glance to right or left. Just before I closed my eyes, I saw cars fleeing into neighboring lanes and heard honkings from all directions. Then I ran through a five-second spot in which I lay covered with bandages in an unknown hospital room, unrecognizable to family and friends alike. When I opened my eyes we had the lane to ourselves. Millicent sank back into the seat and breathed, "Well!"

I saw that my summer experience had begun.

It did not take me long to get things underway. I asked the obvious question, and Millicent replied, "Odin was my grandfather. He came from a seafaring family. His own father was a naval officer. The family home was built so close to the water, you sometimes feel as if you're afloat. We lived there with Grandfather, who took over the place after his father died. During the endless meals we used to have, I would pretend I was sailing in a Spanish galleon."

Millicent did not explain the eye part of Odin's Eye, and after just this much explanation, she withdrew into herself, in reverie, looking straight ahead into the vanishing point. Cars moved unerringly into the lanes on either side of us as we approached them, but she seemed oblivious to this humiliating fact. Left to my own devices, I looked out the window, but there wasn't much to see. A row of trees lined the highway, shielding us from the passing towns, and another row of trees marched up the median strip.

I glanced at Millicent. She was still looking straight ahead, and her face told me no more of what she was thinking than the roadside trees did of what lay beyond. I wondered about her. She and Mother were roughly the same age, in their fifties, and both on the plump side. But Millicent looked more finished in her summer suit than Mother ever would have. That is, if Mother *had* a summer suit and it was as expensive as Millicent's. I could see that Millicent didn't much care what people thought about her, probably because she didn't have to. She was turning out to be okay, maybe even sort of fun; but the trip wasn't very exciting, and it looked as if it would be a long summer. I guess I sighed.

"Odin," said Millicent, "was a monster."

I glanced hurriedly at her. Her eye, the one I could see, was glittering again, but not with humor, and the lines of her face had tightened and hollowed.

"I hated him," she said steadily, "and I hated the house."

I am rarely at a loss for words, but at that moment I found myself without comment or clue to procedure. I couldn't see why she was telling me all this.

"You'll soon discover it—the house reeks of his tyranny," Millicent said. "Odin ruled with an absolute iron hand. He not only ruled my father's life, but my mother's life, and he did his best to rule mine." Then she began to look really sad. "He almost ruined poor old Lummie," she said at last. "I was once engaged to him, but Odin loathed him and eventually broke it up."

I started to ask a pointed question, and I saw myself facing a large placard: DON'T BE RASH. I reconsidered.

"Lummie's an unusual name," I observed.

"Oh, well," said Millicent. "His name is Robert L'Hommedieu. His father was lost early on at sea, but Lummie and his mother continued to live next door to us. In straitened circumstances. Lummie was part of the neighborhood gang. We were all barbarians, of course, and we called him Bobby LaHommydoo. At some point he visited his father's family, and they told him his name meant 'man of God,' and insisted he pronounce it correctly. 'Lummadee*yer*!' he shouted at us when he got home. 'Lummadee*yer*.' Naturally we called him Lummie. Everyone still does, and no one remembers anymore that he is a man of God."

"Mother says he's turned up again," I blurted out, and then realized that this was not exactly tactful, but Millicent didn't bat an eye.

"He'll be there tonight," she said calmly. "He's asked to stay at Odin's Eye for several weeks while he works on some project at the military base up there. He's in communications, and I believe he's way up at the top. He's very bright. He started as a cryptologist —codes and ciphers," she explained unnecessarily.

"And now that the field is so highly technical, I gather he's into all kinds of classified information." Millicent looked troubled. "I can't imagine why he wants to come back to Odin's Eye. It can't have many happy memories for him."

I did not feel qualified to comment on Lummie's return. After a little silence, I retreated onto what I hoped was safer ground.

"My grandfather worked on a secret decoding machine during the war," I observed. But even though I was fascinated by *her* grandfather, Odin Fogelsbee, she showed no interest whatever in mine. There was more silence, but finally Millicent said pleasantly, "Cicely's a pretty name. It reminds me of a pot of—"

"Herbs," I groaned.

"Sweet Cicely," she commented. "Parsley. There's an antique shop in Nova Scotia called Sweet Cicely." None of which information elevated my spirits. Millicent didn't notice my depression, however, and I doubted that she even had her mind on what she was saying, or at least she'd have left out the reference to parsley. I could just hear it, "Old Parsley Barrels" echoing through the high school corridors.

"I need to get back to Odin's Eye as soon as I can," Millicent said. "The other guests are all arriving late this afternoon, and Lummie's bringing someone for dinner. A woman," she added quietly.

At this interesting juncture, Millicent turned off the road and, with a sweeping gesture, into a parking lot. Thus it was that I had the first luncheon of my life in a quaint New England inn. I ordered sweetbreads, because I'd always wondered what they were. They were delicious.

"Do you *know* what sweetbreads are?" asked Millicent, a gleam in her eye.

"Later," I said defensively. "In about five years." Millicent's eyes began to glitter once more, then she laughed, harder and harder, and finally tears rolled down her cheeks. I began to like her.

When we finally arrived, Odin's Eye turned out to be a rambling old place, shingled and weatherbeaten, perched like a gull on the very edge of the water. Two wings, three rooms each, spread out on either side of its elongated body. Cicely's father, it turned out, had had them added so that everybody in his family could look out to sea. Crazy as the place looked from the outside, it now made a nice boarding house, every room with a view and its own little spot of porch, even its own entrance from the garden at the rear.

Millicent and I entered the house from the garden, into a passageway that gave access to the kitchen and the living room. We walked through the kitchen, where various articles of Smithsonian interest seemed on easy speaking terms and the dishwasher, refrigerator, and electric stove stood isolated and shunned. The kitchen opened into the dining room, the dining room onto a porch, and that onto a narrow grassy strip ending in a seawall and, beyond, the water. Dropping my bags, I walked out to the seawall and examined the bay, which was full of boats. Across the water, the opposite shore was dimly lined with buildings and trees, and to my right, seaward, a bridge spanned the bay. On the left and just beyond Odin's Eye, a jetty—a miscellaneous heap of stones and lurching wooden piles—stuck out into the water. I stood there for a while, and then I turned around and looked back at the house.

A wide porch covered the whole front of the house, including the wings. The middle part of the house was two stories high, with windows overlooking the bay, and each side of it abutted into a central peak. In the middle of the peak was the EYE.

A strange configuration of the roof gave the large round window an eyebrow, and a round shutter, pulled up, provided a brooding lid. In the center of the window, a dark glass pupil, perhaps five inches in diameter and edged with a brass rim, gazed over my head and out to sea.

It was absolutely the most gruesome thing I had ever seen, that cold, bloodless, staring eye. Suddenly the glass shifted, moving outward and slightly to the right toward me, and then to my horror, the whole eye slowly tilted downward until it pinned me in its vision. I stood riveted to the spot, balanced on the seawall, unable to yell for help or even to scream, as Odin's terrible Eye moved and focused on me.

"Dear God in heaven," I heard Millicent whisper hoarsely from the porch. "I forgot to close Grandfather's Eye. He'd *kill* me!"

— THREE

I'm of a scientific turn of mind, not much interested in superstition or the spectral, but the grisly Eye and Millicent's terrified utterance from the porch came close to undoing me. Millicent dropped the chair she was unfolding with a thud, and this brought me to my senses.

Gimbals, I thought, taking a less panicked look at the Eye. A gyroscope. And then, seeing that Millicent was going inside, I hastily climbed the porch steps and followed her in.

One of the porch doors opened directly into the living room, and as we crossed toward a staircase at the back, I saw a congregation of wicker chairs, lamps, and tables of a long-gone era. Bookshelves were crammed into every last bit of wall space. A door at one side led off, presumably, to the wing, and at the other side, a wide archway, with a shadowy figurehead above it, opened onto the dining room. The stairway, when we reached it, swayed a little under our feet, by which I gathered that although Odin's Eye had been standing for some seventy-five years, it was not necessarily destined to do so for all time. Still the house was not what I would call a rattletrap, as Mother had said, and I liked it, because it was full of atmosphere and books. A little hallway upstairs opened into Odin's chamber, and, like an ophthalmologist, I made straight for the Eye, and knelt down to examine it.

It was a simple gimbal as I had thought, concentric rings suspended at right angles, which allowed the Eye to move in two planes at the same time. I observed that the pupil, a convex lens, was actually the end of a missing telescope. The brass rim of the lens was fitted into the window glass with some sort of rubbery adhesive, so that the lens on the outside, except for the rim, was smooth with the glass. On the inside of the window, the rim extended about an inch and was threaded so that a telescope, or spyglass if you wanted to call it that, could be screwed onto it. It was an ingenious device, but if all you wanted to do was look out across the bay, why not use a good pair of binoculars? Why this bizarre Eye?

Millicent was busily untying some ropes above my head, and I saw that she was about to lower the round shutter. I pulled the window into its frame and bolted it shut, and Millicent let the ropes slither out like anchor chains through a hole in the wall. There was a thump as the shutter closed down.

"Where's the rest of the telescope?" I asked.

"I neither know nor care," Millicent said shortly. "I do not intend ever to have it in the house again. The Eye was Odin's revenge on the Navy, and if it brought him satisfaction, I, for one, never saw any sign of it." She neatly cleated the rope ends, leaving everything shipshape. I waited—an effort—but after a short pause, Millicent continued.

"He was a martinet aboard ship. His men hated him. Eventually the Navy assigned him to some sort of office job, and he retired in a fury. Almost immediately he had a stroke, which paralyzed one side and blinded that eye."

Millicent walked over and sat on the bed.

"I was sixteen when Odin had his stroke, and immediately following that, I was sent off to one of those awful finishing schools. After my mother died a year or so later, I came back only in the summers, but even then he refused to see me, though he continued to issue orders like the tyrant he was. I actually saw very little of him until I had graduated from college; then for a few years he did relent. But I was already working in New York, and came home rarely. Lummie saw more of Odin than I did; he even lived at Odin's Eye for a short while after his own house burned down. I daresay it wasn't a very warm relationship between them, even though by that time, Lummie and I were engaged."

I tried to get all this into my head at once. Millicent was looking around the room, almost as if she hadn't ever seen it before, or at least not for a very long time.

"I clean up here just once a year, and I was doing it yesterday. I forgot to close the window. The glass glazes over with salt spray, and Grandfather used to throw a proper fit if the shutter was left open. He could look out the other windows, of course, and watch the bay."

"Did *he* build the Eye?" I asked. Millicent shook her head. "A warped, twisted friend of his, Peter Kugle, devised it and built it into the house. He was younger than Odin, a shipbuilder, a brilliant man, but a poor companion for him, I think. I never liked Peter, and I never understood why he was attracted to Odin. I suspect that he took the telescope with him the day Odin died. The housekeeper thought so. I certainly didn't want it back."

"Was Odin an astronomer?" I asked.

"My word, no," said Millicent. "He only used the telescope to spy on Navy ships. He'd always been a stickler for procedure, and Peter's invention allowed him to keep an eye on the crews."

I couldn't help but feel sorry for Millicent. She looked so unhappy, reliving the past this way, and yet I think she wanted to talk about it—maybe to somebody like me who was in no position to comment. I often serve this function, although I think people forget and give out more information sometimes than they intend to.

"The base is up the bay from us," Millicent went on, "and even after the war years, there was a constant parade of naval craft in and out. As the ships passed in front of the house, Odin would open the Eye and rake them with his glass. He'd send in reports of any breaches of procedure he saw, of course. Once, during a hurricane, one of the naval ships moored out in front of the house. You can see the buoy out there."

I looked and spotted a sort of cream-colored, flat-topped cylinder about halfway across the bay.

"The ship broke loose during the storm," Millicent continued, "and they had a hairy time of it. But Grandfather had a ball, watching all the confusion. His report must have made a lot of people cringe."

Nice guy, I thought, and looked around me. Matting covered the floor, but it was a graceless room. All the rough timbers were exposed, though the outside walls were roughly paneled in random-length boards. Odin's weatherbeaten old furniture stood stiffly at attention: a cot-like bed, a chest of drawers, a plain table, and two captain's chairs on rollers. I didn't have much trouble imagining that crippled old man; the room, bare as it was, was full of him.

"He sat up here for over ten years after his stroke," Millicent said, "watching for ships, and pouncing on them with the Eye. Except for that miserable Peter Kugle, he was without any friends at all. I never knew of anyone else coming here except the housekeeper. I was an only child, and when Grandfather died, Odin's Eye was left to me. After I broke with Lummie, I didn't come back for a while, but I finally decided to open it up in the summertime."

Millicent didn't mention now, nor had she brought up at any time, Peter Kugle's murder or the circumstances of her grandfather's death. All kinds of whispered questions lingered in that place.

Millicent started for the door. "We'd better get out of here," she said. "I want to establish you in your quarters. I've put you next to me in the left wing."

I looked around once more. If I saw my mother holding up her hand and saying, "Cicely, don't," I ignored it, as I sometimes do. She has her life and I have mine, and the trick is to know which one the stop sign applies to. My curiosity was aroused, and with curiosity, you might just as well give in to it and find out what you need to know. A mystery lay in this room, and I *had* to know what it was all about.

"I'd like to live up here," I blurted out.

"Right in the Eye?" Millicent stopped in the doorway, incredulity, to say the least, on her face.

"It's—interesting up here," I explained lamely.

Millicent hesitated.

"It would serve him right," she said, finally. "Odin the All-Father. And his All-Seeing Eye." She thought for a moment. "And now an All-Mother. An All-Mother who sees everything." And she laughed, not as if anything were particularly funny, but as if fate had suddenly played into her hands.

I thought of Lummie and this woman he was bringing to Odin's Eye.

"What am I supposed to see?" I asked uneasily.

"I don't know, Cicely," she said slowly. "I don't know what the Eye will see." Then she looked sad and troubled. "I don't know what it has already seen, but I know that we must not close our eyes." I honestly thought Millicent was asking for help.

I am a detective at heart, as Mother well knows. During the day, while Millicent and I sat cooped up in the car, I had instinctively watched her eyes glitter, her hands tighten on the wheel, and I knew something was wrong. Now I began to wonder if she'd decided she could use me, another pair of eyes, to watch. To find out why Lummie had come back. And why he was bringing a woman with him. And what had happened twenty-five years ago.

Then again, maybe I *wasn't* up here in the role of sleuth. Just Cicely Barrows, aide-de-camp. Perhaps all that I'd actually heard was Millicent's cry for help. And then I said to myself that there was nothing wrong with helping a friend in distress. That's what I thought Millicent had turned out to be—a friend.

"I'll go and get your sheets and things," Millicent said at last. "If you really want this room." When I nodded yes, she left.

I walked over to the Eye and, taking hold of the shutter ropes, pulled them in. The eyelid opened, and I knelt down again in front of the glass and looked out.

Right beside the seawall was a boat, and in the boat was a boy who offered, on first glance, a lot more than Bertie Custis ever did. He could have hollered and upset the boat when the Eye opened and focused on him, but he didn't. He just sat there, holding the oars in a steadying position in the water, and looked upward in obvious interest. I unbolted the window and opened it on its vertical rods.

"How does it work?" he called. "I've always wondered."

"Gimbal," I called back.

"Really? Can I come up and see it? I know Miss Fogelsbee. In fact, I came down to see her." He rowed toward the shore, and then the seawall hid him, but he must have beached the boat, because I heard the crunch of gravel. Then his legs crawled over the seawall like a crab, followed by the rest of him. He was mostly legs and arms, but someone had made him stand up straight and walk all in one piece, which is more than I can say for the creeps at school. His face didn't have anything remarkable about it. Blue eyes and a grin. Freckles. Sort of sandy hair. He was older than I was, but not too much. I was heartened to note as he came marching up the porch steps that he didn't look like much of a ballet dancer. I think he would have dismissed Bertie and his pliés with hardly a glance.

Then I heard him come upstairs. When he walked into Odin's room, it was with his hand very formally and correctly extended.

"I'm Geoff Weygand," he said, looking at me with what I hoped was a pleased smile.

"Cicely Barrows," I responded. I expected a horticultural comment on the origins of my name, but he got right down to the business of the Eye.

"My Dad's in the Coast Guard," he said. "The Admiral was gone before he joined up, but he says the men still point out Odin's Eye. Must have shaken them up, all right."

Just then Millicent appeared, what you could see of her, tottering under a tower of blankets and sheets. I got hastily to my feet, but my guest rushed to her rescue and deposited the load on the cot.

"Cicely?" queried Millicent with a startled look at Geoff. "In your bedroom?"

"Call it a studio," I suggested. "It's all a matter of semantics."

"Well," she said, and that settled it, to my relief. "I talked to your mother, Geoff," she added, and here the conversation became confused.

"Cicely," Geoff mused. "You sound just like a pot of herbs." I knew it! Delayed reaction, that's all.

"I suppose Cicely's better than Fleabane," I groaned. "Or Parsley. But not much."

"I hoped you might be able to give me some time this summer." Millicent to Geoff.

"Of course." Geoff to Millicent.

"Geoffrey sounds like the Wars of the Roses." Geoff directed this to me.

"About three days a week, general handyman." Millicent talked into the pile of bed linen, which she was sorting.

"I like it," I said, meaning the name, but thinking about the handyman arrangements.

"Call me Geoff." Geoff to me. "Monday-Wednesday-Friday all right?" Geoff to Millicent.

Millicent, nodding. "Fine."

"Do you have the scope that fits onto this thing?" Geoff asked suddenly.

"*No,*" said Millicent sharply. "And I will not, under any circumstances, have it in this house again." Geoff glanced at me. Then, as Millicent left, he shrugged his shoulders and shook his head. He placed one of the captain's chairs in front of the window and then stood back and studied it.

"The Admiral probably used a refractive telescope," he said with authority.

"Reflective," I said.

"Don't believe he could have managed the viewer from the side at that height," Geoff said. "Being paralyzed and all. It must have been a refractive telescope."

I couldn't imagine that Odin would have been satisfied with a refractive glass, fuzzy and inaccurate as they are reputed to be. "Reflective," I said again.

Geoff looked at me sternly, but respectfully. "Let's have an argument," he said.

My heart leaped up.

— Four

"My boat! The tide's got it!" yelled Geoff, his voice cracking. He dashed out the door and down the stairs, shaking the house. I opened Odin's Eye, horizontally this time, and watched Geoff streak across the grass strip and vault two-handed over the seawall. Then he waded into the sea, churning it as he swam, clothes and all, after his boat. He dragged it to shore, got in, and rowed off with what dignity he could under the circumstances, though he did salute me with an oar as he passed out of sight.

I'd thought, from all Mother had hinted, that I was going to have a spartan summer, in the company of those for whom the whole subject of boys and sex are of little, or past, interest, or even viewed with hostility. I hadn't expected Geoff. I walked rather thoughtfully down to the kitchen, where I found Millicent confronting an enormous piece of meat laid out on the wooden table.

"We tend to eat rather esoterically here," she observed. "Almost everyone likes to cook, and we have a lot of ethnic and gourmet dinners. However, I thought since this was your first night, you might prefer something a little more conservative."

"If that's a round steak," I said, "do let me pound it. I'm practiced in the art." Millicent laughed.

"We could switch to steak teriyaki," she said, "if that would be more to your taste."

In between the usual chores, table-setting, and the washing of lettuce, I watched the preparations with great interest. I was plotting a new and revolutionary regime for my return home, and I had already discovered that lettuce must be shaken dry. I'd been sent out to stand on the seawall and wave the lettuce basket in the air, and as I did so, I thought how great the difference was between Millicent's world and ours. Hers had more vistas.

"Cocktail hour is on the porch," Millicent said. "I like to have as much of the dinner as possible prepared beforehand, so we don't have to keep jumping up and running to the kitchen. There are some things that have to be done at the last minute, of course, and sometimes the cooking is an integral part of the dinner. Then we're *all* in the kitchen."

Later I sat on the porch steps and watched the company gather. They greeted each other so warmly that they had to have known each other for a long time, and they settled themselves into the various chairs and recliners as if *they* were also old friends. Then they looked around and exchanged glances with each other.

"I thought Lummie was going to be here?" one of

them said, and Millicent shrugged. More exchange of glances. Then they focused on me.

I sipped my white grape juice. I guess I could have had sherry, but I was still under the influence of Polonius. I waited rather shyly, wondering what they would say. I needn't have worried, because almost at once they included me into their conversation with what I have always assumed civility to be. Civility is not a quality that shows up often in the humdrum of family existence. When they weren't looking, I set in to study them.

Mayne Cooper was almost my favorite, though out of loyalty, I put Millicent first. The others called her Mayne, but when I called her Miss Cooper, no one suggested that I do otherwise. She was absolutely the most gracious, charming lady I ever saw, and she was still pretty, in a delicate, faded sort of way. She had been everywhere in the world. By the end of the cocktail hour, I figured she was as comfortable on top of a camel as she was riding in first-class accommodations on the Orient Express. Not because she was being stiff-upper-lipped about the camel, either—she was simply oblivious to the vicissitudes of life. Everything turned out to be *most* interesting, or beautiful, and the stars turned on and off in her eyes as easily as the hall light at home and about as often.

I'd have been more in awe of the one in the reclining chair, Regina Peppers, if she hadn't looked so tired. She had nodded in an interested way at me and told me to call her Regina. She was a friend of Millicent's from New York, an author, and she'd just finished a book and got it off to the publishers, which was probably the reason for her fatigue. She was wearing a russet-colored, turtleneck sweater and brown slacks. With her bright, rather birdlike eyes, and her slick black hair, she looked like a robin.

Then there was Aunt Tattie, nobody's aunt, but she had taught three generations of children in the area, Lummie and Millicent among them, and she had the quiet confidence that comes from having done just that and not having fallen apart in the process. She sat plumply in her chair and tatted, hence her name, and although she was a generation or more older than the others, she didn't miss one single syllable of the conversation. She looked at me with a practiced eye and asked me what my favorite book was.

"*Kristin Lavransdatter*," I said. "Mother says I talk like her." I was expecting the worst, but to my surprise, everyone nodded in approval. It was apparent that in this company I could have talked like Matthew, Mark, Luke, and John, and no one would have known the difference. I was thinking better and better of the summer ahead.

"Millicent," Regina asked, cocking her head and listening as if she were locating a worm in the front lawn, "was your grandfather's name *really* Odin? I know that the god had only one eye. Is the window simply a coincidence?"

The Norse gods were just about my first loves, and

I'd been wanting to ask the same question, but Mother's strong admonition, probably deserved, not to be nosy, was still on my mind.

"His name was Odin all right," said Millicent, "but I doubt that he knew one single thing about his namesake. He wasn't much of a reader. I can't imagine he'd have had the least interest in the gods and their goings-on. After the Eye was put in, my mother, who was amused by the whole business, began to call him the All-Father—which he never understood, of course—and she tried to name the house Asgaard after the abode of the gods. But that name didn't work."

"Asgaard was supposed to be a happy place," I observed, and Millicent gave me a shrewd look.

"Odin the All-Father," Regina murmured. "I never thought Odin was overly effective, though. After all, the ice giants came and did Asgaard in."

"Right," said Millicent, a little sadly. "It all ended in disaster." Aunt Tattie looked up from her handwork and studied Millicent from over the top of her glasses. Somehow a pall fell over the group, until Miss Cooper began to talk with rapture about Norway and the fjords. She'd sailed up to see the midnight sun, and even though this has been going on for eons, I guess, you'd have thought the firmament had put on a spectacle one time more just out of kindness to her. Anyway, we all forgot about Odin's Eye.

The cocktail hour seemed to go on too long. No one wanted any more sherry, and the little canapes were all eaten up. I guessed we were waiting for Lummie. I'm sure all the others were listening for a car or a door opening, as I was. At last Millicent said, "Well—" in an indeterminate voice, and they all got to their feet. We gathered around the venerable oak table in the dining room, and two places simply remained vacant, one of them at the head of the table, opposite Millicent.

"Cicely is interested in the Russian ballet," said Millicent with a perfectly poker face. I opened my mouth to protest, but Mayne Cooper threw up her hands in excitement, exclaimed, "How interesting!" and rushed on to describe the ballet in Moscow or Leningrad, I forget which, and her visit to the Imperial ballet school. Then they all began to discuss the ballet and describe various dancers they had seen. The conversation went on to different kinds of ballet and then to modern dance. It was all so new and authentic that if it hadn't been for the several hours of sea air I'd breathed, I'd have forgotten to eat my steak teriyaki. I almost forgot about Lummie.

Everyone heard the sounds of someone entering the kitchen and stopped talking. This tall, gorgeous woman came in, followed by Lummie. He pulled out a chair for her and then sat down at the head of the table as if he owned it.

"I'd like to introduce Olive Plumtree," Lummie said. "She's working with me this summer at the base."

Olive Plumtree! Shock sat me bolt upright. *"But Mother—"* I started to say, when I glanced at Millicent. If ever anyone ever saw tragedy, bound, gagged, and imprisoned, it was there on her face. For once I had sense enough to hold my tongue.

Lummie went suavely around the table making and receiving introductions, until he came to me, when he stopped dead.

It was a pure case of hate at first sight.

I guess there was nothing outwardly wrong with Lummie. He had light-brown hair and a mustache, and was tanned and nattily dressed. He was Millicent's generation—the age of my parents—and his face was a little jowly and hollowed in at the cheeks. But he gave me an eerie feeling. A part of him seemed to be in hiding. I thought of my father's face, lined and seasoned, but open, and I wondered why Lummie looked so closed up and so haunted. I didn't like him, and all I could think of was, Millicent still cares for him after all these years—*this?*

"Cicely Barrows," said Millicent quietly, and with a now frozen face. "Lummie, you've heard me talk about my cousin Caroline. Cicely is her daughter, and she's spending the summer here, to give me a hand."

Lummie obviously found this news as distasteful as if a stray cat had squeezed through the screen door and jumped, fleas and all, into his lap. "All summer?" he asked rudely, and I heard a faint "Why, *Lummie!*" from Miss Cooper.

I glanced at Millicent and saw for the second time that day the gimlet look in her face.

"Yes, she is, Lummie," she said, "and she's staying in Odin's room, inside the Eye."

"Inside the Eye?" Lummie croaked hoarsely, and I was sure I saw fear in his face. Then he exploded, "Millicent, *no!*"

There was a strange sound, a suppressed laugh. Everyone at the table turned to Olive Plumtree.

She was startlingly beautiful. Her wavy, graying hair was cut short, exposing the high cheekbones of her rather feline face. She was as aloof and remote as a lioness, and she looked at the guests around the table with the cat-like sleepiness that is nevertheless alert to the slightest movement. Her tawny eyes fastened on me. They widened and stared, then closed, and the laugh, deep in her throat, rumbled on, more like a purr than anything else.

Millicent was absolutely furious. "I'll put my guests where I please, Lummie," she spit at him.

"In that case," said Lummie coldly, "perhaps you would be willing to put Olive up for tonight, since you seem to have an extra room?" Millicent, white with fury, didn't answer. I waited to hear Olive protest that she would go to a motel. Instead, she pulled out a cigarette and lit it, though she hadn't yet eaten a bite, and looked around the table from half-closed eyes. There was a dreadful silence.

Mayne Cooper, leaping into the breach, picked up the conversation where it had broken off earlier and gracefully reestablished it. But in the middle of a sentence she stopped.

"Olive," she said, puzzled. "I've seen you somewhere before. I *know* I have." Olive blew a cloud of smoke slowly into the air, and her eyes went to little slits. She didn't answer.

Millicent and I cleared the dishes, and she helped me stow them in the dishwasher. "This once," she said, "so you'll know what to do." I gathered—correctly—that cleaning up was to be one of my chores.

"Mother knew this Olive Plumtree in high school," I said finally. Millicent, wiping off the kitchen table, stopped in the middle of a wide swath.

"How very odd," she said.

"She said that Olive Plumtree hasn't been heard of since."

Millicent slowly resumed her wiping motions.

"Would that it were so, Cicely," she said gravely. "Would that it were so." She straightened. Then she crushed the dishcloth into a ball, looking down at it without apparently seeing it.

"Why is she working with Lummie? What are they up to?" she asked, so softly that I didn't know whether she was talking to me or not. "Who is she?" and so low that I could scarcely hear her, "What terrible business has she dragged Lummie into . . . ?"

My mind answered the question—with another question: Espionage?

— FIVE

The airplane that flew up the bay late in the night must have been droning on for several seconds, but I didn't hear it until its coughing and sputtering woke me up suddenly. I sat upright in bed, my heart thumping. Somebody out there in the darkness was in terrible trouble, and no one could do one single thing to help. The engine died and then started with a desperate roar, only to break, cough, and sputter again. The plane seemed to pass by the house, though I was not sure of this, but I heard a final scream of the motor and then silence. I ran to the window, shaking with fear, but I couldn't see anything at all, nothing from any of my windows, though I raced from one to the other. No sound, nothing but blackness.

I wondered what to do. I listened, but there was no stirring in the house—unbelievable that no one had heard the airplane fall but me! Perhaps, being upstairs, I had heard the engine more clearly. At home I would have dashed into my parents' room, or in earlier years, wakened my older brother or sister. But I didn't know these people in Odin's Eye very well—did you rush madly downstairs in the middle of the night, pounding on doors, crying alarm, when there was absolutely nothing to be seen or heard? I didn't know where the plane had gone down, or even if it had.

I opened my bedroom door and listened again, and then I walked partway downstairs and peered over the banisters into the dark living room. I heard the scurrying of mice in the fireplace—Mother was right about them—but there was no other sound at all. I walked all the way down the steps, and even ventured into the dining room in order to check the hallways of both wings, but the doors were all closed, and I just couldn't rush up and bang on them. In the end I stole back upstairs and sat at my side window, trying desperately to see something, anything, and at last I pushed the Eye open and sat partly out on the sill, staring into the darkness and waiting.

It was fifteen minutes past three by my wristwatch.

Finally, up the bay I caught sight of a tiny light, bobbing and often disappearing, but it seemed to be moving from the shore into the center of the bay. I thought maybe someone in a small boat had gone out to look around, someone who had also heard the death throes of the airplane. And then there was another light, though it was hard to be sure where. Lights on the water, at night, can distort distances—at least, that's what I've read. I really didn't know how far away this one was.

A half hour or more must have passed when I heard the beat of a chopper, and presently floodlights pierced the darkness downward, like great feelers probing the water. I knew then that I had been right, that a plane had gone down, and I began to worry. What if John had come home sooner than he intended from the West Coast, and this were *his* plane? I knew this was impossible, and yet . . . There was still no sound from the rest of the house. I would have to wait, to see if the telephone would ring. I knew it wouldn't. I knew I was being childish and dramatic, but I couldn't help it. It was chilly, and I was shaking with cold. I crawled back into bed. I heard another copter, and then, in spite of my worries, although later I couldn't believe that I did, I fell asleep.

In the morning, when I woke up, the first thing I thought was: The telephone didn't ring. I dressed and went downstairs. The guests, still in nightclothes, had gathered on the porch and were looking up the bay with binoculars. Some distance away, a collection of naval craft—one of them, at least, a Coast Guard ship, which I recognized by the slash down its side—were doing a sort of circle dance.

"What *do* you suppose has happened?" Mayne Cooper asked in a wondering, slightly indignant tone, as if there were no excuse for disorder out in the bay so early in the morning. She had on an absolutely elegant negligee, of peach satin and lace, and I wondered if she took it with her to places like Tibet.

Millicent handed me her binoculars. "I think—" I started to say, but at this moment Lummie, followed by Olive Plumtree, drifted out from the dining room and stood beside me to look up the bay.

"What's going on?" Lummie asked.

"I think a plane went down early this morning," I said. "I'm sure I heard it go down." Lummie snatched the binoculars roughly from my hand, and Olive, whirling, pounced on my words.

"What did you say, Cicely?" she asked tensely. "What time was this?"

"A little after three," I answered. "Fifteen minutes after three when I first looked," I said honestly, because the expression on her face brooked no nonsense. Her cat-like eyes, still fixed on my face, narrowed, and then she held out her hand for the binoculars. Lummie was busy looking, but he saw her imperious gesture anyhow, and instantly handed the glasses over. In that one gesture I knew that these two were, as Millicent suspected, into something together, and I also knew who was in charge, and which one we ought to keep an eye on.

Olive and Lummie continued to watch after the rest of us had gone in to prepare our different breakfasts. Millicent stared at the two of them out on the porch with a lowering expression, and scarcely touched her food. I heard Lummie mutter something about the telephone, but since it was in the dining room, they apparently decided not to use it. Presently, to everyone's evident relief, because they all started to talk at once, Lummie and Olive left. Almost immediately, I heard a car backing out on the gravel from behind the garden.

We tuned in to the local radio station, but no mention was made of a downed plane. Millicent went to the telephone and inquired of a neighbor who had a TV, but nothing had been aired.

"It's something military," said Regina with conviction. She was wearing blue slacks and the same russet-colored sweater, but now she looked like a bluebird. I wondered if each day she'd take a clue from Mr. Peterson and go through the whole guide book: tomorrow, gray, black, and white—chickadee; the next day, blue-gray, white with a touch of rose—titmouse; and so forth.

"We won't know a thing unless we can find someone in the service who'll drop a hint," Millicent moaned. "It's simply maddening. If it had been some civilian plane, the news would have been all over the country."

Geoff arrived in great excitement, but he didn't know anything more than we did. His father, who might have been a source of information, was inconveniently out at sea, and his brother, who was also in the Coast Guard, was stationed at a base somewhere and wouldn't be much help, Geoff said. Millicent moaned and groaned all over again.

It was not Geoff's work day, but he helped me with the chores, and then wheedled Millicent into letting me row out in his boat to see what was going on. Well, not exactly wheedled, because Millicent was so pleased to see me go with him that it reminded me forcefully of my mother. She did ask in some concern if it weren't pretty rough for his little boat, but Geoff dismissed her worry with a wave of his hand.

I was born and reared inland. My family is civilian to the core, and I was in awe of both the sea and the military. As we neared the Coast Guard cutter, the ship towered higher and higher out of the water. So did the waves, and to my secret alarm, we began to bounce up and down. I was sitting in the bow, facing Geoff's back as he rowed. I turned from time to time to watch where we were going, and I got really wet as the boat spanked the water. Several Coast Guard launches lolled about, their motors throttled, and I thought, Gosh, wouldn't it be nice to sit securely inside one of them. The waves were hardly rocking them at all.

Suddenly a voice roared out from one of the launches. "You, Geoffrey Weygand, this is restricted area. What are you doing out here, anyway, in this sea? You get the hell back to shore."

The officious, megaphoned voice, which rang out over the water, turned Geoff, who had stopped rowing, from a pleasing tan to a lobster-red. The guy standing up in the launch looked sort of young to me, but he was in uniform and he seemed to have a lot of authority. Geoff was simply furious, though, and he shouted something military about blowing it out of a duffel bag.

"Go on back!" roared the megaphone. "And now, you nerd!"

"It's my brother," said Geoff through clenched jaws. "And he'll blow the whole story to Dad."

There was nothing to do but row back. Geoff was so

mad, and we chopped the water so fast, you'd have thought we were a hydrofoil. About halfway back he stopped rowing.

"Let's find the telescope for Odin's Eye and spy on them," he said with vengeance.

My alarm system went into action. After all, the telescope, much as I privately wanted to see it, was against the law—Millicent's Law—OFF LIMITS.

I have always noticed that if a male has only the faintest idea planted in his mind, he is doomed to follow it. I remember that my brother and some of his buddies years ago dug a man-trap out in the woods. My father pointed out that some innocent wayfarer could walk into it and sprain his ankle. Then he walked down into the woods to take a look at it, and he didn't come back. I was only a little thing at the time, but I knew exactly what had happened.

"He's down in the trap with a sprained ankle," I said. Surprise, surprise. Mother had to drop everything and take care of him for two weeks, and she was fit to be tied.

"Couldn't you have walked *around* it?" she asked.

"The stupid boys dug it right in the path," he answered.

That's the way it is with boys. So, hoping to deflect Geoff, I pointed out, "You're doing exactly what Odin Fogelsbee did. He got mad at the Navy and built a telescope so he could spy on the boats. And here you are, mad at the Navy and spying with a telescope all over again."

"Mad at the *Coast Guard,*" he corrected me. "For God's sake, don't mix up the Coast Guard and the Navy!"

"You're just taking revenge on your brother," I explained patiently. "Like Odin. All he wanted to do was get even." Geoff didn't make the connection.

"Oh, boy," he said with gritted teeth. "I can hardly wait." This tack was not working.

"Millicent doesn't have the telescope," I said, changing course. "She thinks Peter Kugle took it. And he's dead."

"Then we'll go see Nate. That's Peter's son."

"But Millicent said she wouldn't have the telescope in the house," I reminded him. "It's really off limits."

"We're not going to tell her," he said in manful tones.

Maybe we won't be able to find it, I thought, but something told me that that was too easy an out. I figured I was going to have Geoff *and* the telescope, or I wasn't going to have either one.

"We'll row over to Nate's this afternoon," he said. "He lives in the old family place, just a little way from you. You can see his point from your house."

The boat ground to a stop, and Geoff waded to shore and pulled me in, so that I got out dry-shod, although I was soaked otherwise.

There was Lummie all by himself up on the porch, binoculars in hand, and he looked almost as furious as Geoff.

"What were you doing out there?" he shouted at us

as we approached the steps. "Who told you you could go out there?"

Since Lummie didn't know Geoff, I thought he was acting like an awful bully. Either that, or all this show of rage bordered on some sort of panic. At any rate, it didn't make a pretty sight—a professional-looking, middle-aged man shouting at a teenager like that, for no apparent reason. Geoff simply stood up even straighter than usual and looked directly at Lummie.

"Millicent did, if it's any business of yours," Geoff answered shortly, and with no more emotion than swatting a mosquito. I waited for Lummie to blow his stack, but though his face contorted, he seemed to pull himself together instead. He turned abruptly and lifted his binoculars to his eyes again, ignoring us. I presumed the interchange was over, Geoff the clear winner. But I was uneasy. I already didn't like Lummie, and this display of temper raised my hackles. People like Lummie don't swallow defeat: They remember.

Geoff dismissed the whole incident with no more than a shrug. "What a nerd," he muttered as we walked into the dining room. And then he smiled down at me and said, "I'll come around for you after lunch."

I started to say no, because of Millicent, but all at once I thought of Mother, how pleased she'd be that Geoff had turned up and that I was showing a little interest. Besides, I really wanted to see the telescope. We wouldn't have to bring it home, I thought. The ground began to erode beneath my feet.

"Okay," I replied, but only half happy.

— Six

You never can tell about boys. They make a date, like going to Nate's after lunch. Then they go home, and it turns out that a sergeant-major parent has decided it's time to clean the garage. Obviously they can't phone and say, "My mother won't let me out," so they just don't show up. It's only if you happen to pass that way on your bike and see him at hard labor that you know what's happened. So I didn't count on Geoff's coming back.

And I didn't know how to explain to Millicent that we were planning to visit Nate Kugle. I knew she'd go straight from A to B, Kugle to telescope. I decided not to mention it at all as we ate our lunch of avocado stuffed with shrimp, which two items were almost as foreign to my diet at home as bird's-nest soup.

Geoff did show up, however, in what looked like a new pair of Levi's, just as we were finishing our salad, and he said with a winning smile, "Miss Fogelsbee, would you like some fish for dinner? We're going to row over to Nate's point."

Millicent clasped her hands and said, "Lovely!" This

was echoed with such fervency around the table that I didn't know whether it was the promise of fish or the image of my rowing off with Geoff that caused the excitement. I suspected the latter: I was beginning to wonder if I hadn't traded one anxious parent for four more of the same persuasion. Lummie was not there. He had disappeared, and Olive had not been around since breakfast.

Geoff helped me into the boat and pushed it off the shore. Then he leaped into the stern and crawled over the seats to the oars.

I offered to help row, but he seemed so insulted at the idea that I shut up. I couldn't help noticing, though, that we were barreling along on the ebb tide, the wind behind us, and that most of his efforts were expended in simply keeping the prow headed in the right direction.

"Nate used to be an artist," Geoff explained as we neared the point, "and I think he still paints some. Actually, for a number of years, he's fished for a living." Then he hesitated. "He's pretty much out of it now, goes off without warning. He's not dangerous or anything. I suppose he's getting senile, but he hasn't been right for a long time."

"Since his father was murdered?" I asked. Geoff turned around and gave me a quick look.

"Well, yes," he said uncomfortably. "But we're all used to him. He's been hooked on Captain Kidd for years. Even before his father died. He's really lost touch with reality. He goes on and on about finding treasure."

"Well, *is* there any treasure around here?" I asked.

Geoff shrugged and pointed. "Doc Thomas—he lives there, behind Nate—he thinks there's treasure on Nate's point," he answered. "Doc's a mortician from New Jersey. Most of us think he works for the Mafia. He comes up here in the summer, and prowls around with his Geiger counter. Been doing it for thirty years or more, and as far as anyone knows, never found anything."

A lot of peculiar summer people seemed to have gathered around Odin's Eye. When they went home in the fall, they probably just dropped out of local sight and mind. I'd be dropping out of sight eventually, too, and Geoff would pick up where he left off, but I didn't like the idea.

Geoff wasn't thinking about my dropping out of sight. He was still talking about Doc Thomas and Nate.

"Doc's practically torn his own house apart looking for treasure," he continued. "He's wild to get at Nate's. He thinks that pirates hid money in those old fireplaces, and he's always trying to get people to pull chunks out of them. You can see his house now."

A curving seawall and a row of trees partly blocked our view, but behind them I got a glimpse of mowed green lawn and, presently, an imposing summer home. Nate Kugle's point sort of hooked off the end of this property, and Nate's old stone house stood on it, exposed and surrounded by festoons of fishnet.

"Remember, Nate's harmless," said Geoff as we beached the boat. After I got out, he pulled it way up on the shore, probably because he wasn't keen on dunking his new Levi's.

Nate was sitting in his doorway smoking a pipe. You'd expect a fisherman to be ruddy, but Nate looked old and bleached out. The old-man pallor reached up into his hair, which seemed to match it, though he may have been just very blond. Even his blue eyes were faded. He held up a finger as we approached, as if he were hearing voices and didn't want us to disturb them, but Geoff said with easy familiarity, "Hello there, Nate. How're you doing?"

They got right down to the business of fillets, and Nate walked to an ice chest at the side of the house and opened it. He pulled out some fillets, wrapped them up, and Geoff paid him.

Then we sat down on some small barrels outside the front door. I supposed they originally held fish, and I tested mine out of caution before I sat on it; but Geoff plunked himself right down and engaged Nate in pleasant banter about the weather and the state of the sea. Finally he got around to asking him about the Coast Guard activity in the bay. Nate looked secretive and said, "*I* know, *I* know," but divulged nothing. Personally, I wasn't convinced that he knew anything at all.

I had to hand it to Geoff. First he was talking about Nate's father, then about Odin Fogelsbee, and then Odin's Eye, what an old house it was and how spooky the Eye must look from the water. Nate kept muttering and nodding his head. He seemed to be following the conversation all right.

"Have you any idea what happened to the telescope?" Geoff asked smoothly, and I thought he had his hands on it for sure. But the question obviously terrified Nate, and he began to look all around him, peering around the corners of the house as if someone might be hidden there.

"Lummie's back," he whispered. "I saw him. I saw him sitting on Odin's porch," and then he stopped talking altogether. He wouldn't even look up, but sat bent over, his eyes on the ground.

I hardly dared look at Geoff. Fishermen who have lost a big one are often without words for a time. While they reel in the line, it's better not to make too many observations about life. Geoff didn't try another cast, as most fishermen do, and the silence became oppressive.

"Geoff says you paint pictures." I ventured this to Nate, hoping to rouse him a little, and he jumped instantly back into his mind—it was really spooky to see how aware he became. He got to his feet, and we followed him inside his house, where watercolors hung crookedly all over the walls; some were even taped to the chimney of the old stone fireplace.

I had not expected such delicate, almost feminine, paintings, if there are such things, or if it's all right to say so. He had used the barest tints for colors, and all the paintings had a misty, teary look.

"Oh!" I exclaimed, because I thought they were beautiful. Nate became a little agitated, and he kept showing me one after another, excitedly calling, "Here!

Here!" so that I had to dash from one side of the room to the other. The watercolors were mostly scenes of the bay and of houses along the shore. I went with increasing pleasure from picture to picture, but though I think I looked at all of them, I couldn't find one of Odin's Eye.

"I wish I could have one of your paintings sometime, Nate," I said, and I meant it, because I loved his way of giving you just the tiniest hint of what was really there. But I knew artists charged a lot for pictures. The funds Mother had given me were limited, and their specific use was a large section of my departing instructions.

"Come on, Cicely," Geoff said impatiently. "We'd better get back." I felt sorry for him, toting home an empty creel, except for the fillets he'd bought, and I started to follow him; but Nate stealthily pulled on my sleeve and beckoned me toward the back of the room. I wondered what he was going to do—maybe show me some more paintings, or even give me one? I hesitated, but with little tugs and tweaks at my elbow, he ushered me through the door. We entered a den, or a study, with an official but dusty desk under the window and bookcases full of mildewed books. They seemed to be scientific, books of engineering, and I caught sight of one about optics. I assumed they had belonged to Peter Kugle. None of Nate's pictures hung on the walls, none at all, and from the mustiness of the place, I doubted that Nate came in here very often. I began to wonder if maybe he *did* have the telescope hidden away here in his father's study.

There must have been something about the place that disturbed him, because all at once he went off, snatching at my sleeve and putting his face close to mine, talking very fast and in disjointed sentences about Captain Kidd and treasure.

"He can't have it," he warned, pointing out the window toward the mortician's house, but also muttering a lot about his father, Peter Kugle, and once even pulling a book from the bookcase and slamming it on the floor. He talked about Odin's Eye, though I couldn't make sense of what he was saying, and then, all at once, he began to call me Millicent. Geoff stood protectively beside me and murmured, "Don't worry," but I was scared stiff, bottled up with an Ancient Mariner like this. He rambled on, becoming more and more excited.

"Do you want a picture, little lady?" he asked suddenly. I gathered that for some reason, I was no longer Millicent, and in fact he seemed to quiet down. He went over to the desk and produced a piece of paper and a pencil. "I'll send you one," he promised, and pushed the paper at me. I decided that he wanted my name and address, and after a moment's hesitation, I wrote it down, giving my address back home, because I *did* want a painting. Geoff began to steer me out of the room.

"He'll calm down in a minute," he said, "but we'd better get going." We started for the door.

"Wait! Wait!" called Nate, and he rushed over to a closet and flung open the door. He disappeared into it and then reappeared, holding this huge telescope in his arms. He thrust it at me, and in a daze, I took it.

I could see from the threading on the brass rim, and from the missing lens, that it was indeed Odin's famous spyglass. I stood there, clutching it, not knowing what to do. I looked at Geoff. "It's refractive," I said, conceding.

"Gosh, Cicely!" he responded graciously. "Nice going! We've got it!" But my heart sank. I was never so torn in my life. It was such a beautiful instrument, and it was so exciting to have found it, that Millicent's orders sounded downright cruel. I looked back at Nate, and I saw that he was terrified.

"Take it! Take it," he cried. He was shaking all over. "It belongs to *you,* Millicent," he said. "It belongs to Odin's Eye." Then he became really distraught and looked fearfully over his shoulder. "Father stole it!" he hissed at me. "You know he did. He had no right!"

He clawed at my elbow and looked wildly around him.

"Don't show the glass to Lummie, Millicent," he pleaded frantically. "Don't let Lummie see it—no! No!" He put his face close to mine.

"I fear the man of God," he whispered.

— SEVEN

The telescope lay in the bottom of the boat. I had no more ability to stop the course of events than we had to turn the tide. And this was no joke, because Geoff was battling both it and the wind. In spite of his frantic rowing, we were not far from the point where we had set off, and I was afraid if he stopped rowing for even a second, we'd be swept out to sea. This time he gratefully accepted my offer of help, and with both of us rowing, we got ourselves safely to port.

Then we had the problem of getting the telescope into Odin's Eye without anyone seeing us. Geoff pulled up to our seawall and sent me off on a scouting expedition. Lummie was no longer on the porch, and the binoculars were gone, but a smaller pair of bird glasses sat on the table. I called "Millicent?" several times, and receiving no answer from anyone, trained the glasses on the beach. Far up the shore, picking their way over the rocks, I spotted the four ladies. I walked up the left wing porch to Lummie's room and casually looked through his window, but he wasn't there.

I signaled to Geoff, and with no trouble whatsoever,

we got the telescope upstairs and screwed onto the Eye. The telescope pulled out into three sections, by simple friction rather than ratchet—this to make it easier for Odin to focus. The eyepiece, of etched brass, was a true work of art, and the wood of the shaft was so silky and polished that I wanted to rub it against my cheek. No wonder Peter Kugle wanted his telescope back!

Geoff wheeled Odin's chair to the window, and you could almost see the old man sitting there. Everything was so exact that he could have trained on any action in the bay, at least within range of the instrument.

As soon as the telescope was ready, Geoff sat down and adjusted the eyepiece. "Oh, boy," he murmured. "Neat!" And then with vengeful glee, "I've got them!"

I was dying to look through the telescope myself, but my conscience was giving me fits. For the moment, I was actually glad that Geoff, in his frenzy to get even with his brother, seemed to have forgotten all about me.

I sat in Odin's other chair and read a book. It was one of a stack that Millicent had brought up when she was furnishing my room with dresser scarves and lamps. Books are a necessary part of the environment, a fact that Millicent understood without my having to point it out. The book I'd picked up was *Three Men in a Boat* by Jerome K. Jerome, in dull red covers, and sprinkled through with hilarious little sketches. Geoff was so lost in *his* world of revenge that he probably didn't even hear me giggling away.

Pretty soon I became aware that Geoff was dancing

about and making gestures of conquest. It turned out that he'd caught the crew of his brother's boat, and his brother, in some dereliction of duty—I think they all took a swig from a flask. I figured it must have been chilly out there, hour after hour, in an open boat, and I couldn't get excited about it.

"It's probably coffee or something," I pointed out.

"Ha!" said Geoff, and he rubbed his hands and did another war dance. It looked like blackmail to me, though I tried to show some appreciation of it. He went back to the telescope, and I to my reading.

Suddenly he said, "Hey!" in such a startled tone that I dropped my book. "What's Lummie doing way out there on the jetty?"

"Where is he?" I asked. I couldn't stand it any longer. "Let me see," I demanded, and Geoff made way for me at the telescope.

I couldn't understand why Geoff took the *fact* of that powerful telescope so calmly. I could see as clearly across the bay as if I were sitting just offshore in a boat. There was a military installation over there, and I could see the men in their white uniforms, the dock, and various crafts tethered to it, though I suppose Geoff would have used a more nautical expression. I could even see all the boats rocking in unison with the waves. Then I looked at the Coast Guard circle, and I saw at once that they were diving for the plane, not that I hadn't figured that out already.

"Have you found Lummie?" asked Geoff impatiently, and I hastily trained the telescope on the stone jetty up the bay from our house. At first all I saw were the birds, but suddenly I glimpsed Lummie sitting way out at the end, hidden by the pilings. He was watching the Coast Guard operations through his binoculars.

"What's he *doing* out there?" Geoff asked.

"Well, watching the Coast Guard, I guess," I answered, not pointing out that Geoff had been doing exactly the same thing himself a minute before.

"But *why?*" Geoff asked in concerned tones. "What business is it of his?"

I shook my head. "Why did Nate say he feared the man of God?" I asked. "That's Lummie, of course."

"I don't know very much about it," Geoff said. "Millicent and Lummie were engaged. Lummie broke it off, but everyone thinks Odin was at the bottom of it. Millicent, they say, never forgave her grandfather. I don't think anyone knows what happened over here, but Odin and Lummie had a big fight. The housekeeper heard angry voices and thought they were fighting about Millicent, but she wasn't able to come up with any of the actual conversation. In the middle of it, though, Odin had a second stroke. Lummie called the housekeeper, and she ran upstairs, but Odin died before they could get help."

"Where was Millicent?" I asked.

"In New York. She hadn't lived here for years, just came back occasionally to check on things."

"But what happened to Peter Kugle?" I persisted.

"The housekeeper called him, and he went right over to Odin's Eye. It was established that he went home afterward, though they were never able to get much out of Nate. After Peter was found murdered—they discovered his body down on the shore the next morning—Nate went all to pieces and had to be hospitalized. He was gone for a long time." During this explanation, Geoff looked increasingly uncomfortable, and I was getting this awful feeling in my stomach.

"Did Lummie do it?" I asked in a squeaky little voice. "Or Nate?"

"No one knows," said Geoff. "Nate had never been violent, and nobody could really believe *he* did it. Lummie, of course, was suspect, but in the end he was completely cleared. They've never really discovered a motive for the murder."

I thought about this for a while. "Peter Kugle wouldn't have had anything to do with the engagement, I wouldn't think. Where did Lummie go? Did he wait to tell Millicent he'd broken off with her?"

"He took off right after Odin's death. At the inquest he had witnesses all up and down the line, showing where he had been. He never even waited for Millicent, just left her this awful letter, I guess. He completely avoided her at the inquest. And he hasn't been back since. His work used to take him to the base some, but as far as I know, he's never been back there, either."

"If Odin didn't like Lummie, maybe he had good reason," I observed. Geoff grunted assent. He took my place at the telescope and watched the bay a while longer.

"People around here didn't like Lummie," Geoff said. "Millicent's a nice person, and she had a raw deal from him, most of the neighbors think."

"Millicent blames Odin, though," I said.

"There's a lot that's never been answered," Geoff said. "Why Nate is so scared of Lummie, and all. I've never seen Lummie before, but it took me about two seconds to figure *him* out."

I didn't feel like reading anymore.

Suddenly Geoff, who was moving the eye around, started, then focused the glass on some point that had caught his attention.

"There's something else crazy out there," he said. "There's a little motor launch hanging around that old buoy."

"What's crazy about that?" I asked

"You'd know if you'd ever been out there," he said. "The gulls land on the buoy, and it stinks. No one goes near if if they don't have to."

"Let me see," I said. Geoff moved over, and I focused Odin's Eye on the buoy. There were three men in the boat—I thought that was appropriate—but then I jumped nearly out of my skin. A fourth person came up out of the cabin.

"It's Olive Plumtree," I said. "She's in the boat."

"Who?" Geoff asked. I explained, and he looked uneasy.

"Why did Lummie come back anyhow?" he asked. "And why would he bring this Olive Plumtree with him? Why would he want to hurt Millicent like that?"

"Olive's really beautiful," I said. "But I don't think she's Lummie's girlfriend or anything like that."

"Why?"

I didn't know why. Perhaps because I agreed with Geoff that Lummie was such a nerd. Olive Plumtree was simply too much for him. Something wasn't fitting together.

"Millicent wants me to watch Olive Plumtree," I said slowly. "I guess its because Lummie's work is so hush-hush—military satellites and things. And, well—I think Millicent's worried about Olive, whether she's sort of a—secret agent or something—and has Lummie involved . . ." I suggested this, faltering a lot, because thinking something and actually saying it out loud were two different things, and hearing it in my own voice was pretty scary.

"Well, gee whiz, Cicely," Geoff said promptly. He looked really pleased. Maybe the prospect of a spy in our midst added spice to a dull summer of mowing grass and taking the garbage to the town dump. And in that moment it occurred to me that it would be nice to have a partner. Most detectives do, to keep up their spirits and to fetch things, and also to ask questions of, which helps to clarify the issues. Without really knowing it, we made a pact.

"I don't think either Lummie or Millicent should know about the telescope," Geoff observed after a moment.

"Or Olive," I said. Geoff looked uneasy.

"We'd better hide it," he said. "But you're going to

have to keep watch when I'm not here." Out of deference to Millicent, I did not commit myself.

We rather soberly took the telescope apart. For want of a better place, we slipped it in the leg of a pair of my jeans, which we then pinned together at the foot and hung up in the closet. Nobody that I ever heard of hangs up jeans, and if I were trying to find a long, skinny telescope, a bulging leg hanging up in the closet would be the first place I'd look. But Geoff thought it was a perfect hiding place.

Then he had to leave. His mother needed him, he explained. On a hunch, I asked if he had to clean out the garage, and he looked grave, as if he had suddenly discovered he was talking to an oracle.

I sat down in my chair again, my book in my lap, and worried. In spite of the sleuth business, I wished that we'd never found the telescope. Millicent hadn't minced words about having it in the house; I'd heard her give two pretty direct orders.

On the other hand, I'd elected to live up in Odin's room precisely because I *did* want to know what had happened at Odin's Eye, and I thought the secret was to be found up here. In spite of Millicent, the Eye and the telescope fascinated me. What *was* going on out in the bay? I wanted to know that, too. I sat there thinking for a lot longer than I usually do.

I had noticed, with an increasingly queasy feeling, that when I was in Odin's room, as I was now, the Eye seemed to be looking at me, no less than when it had discovered me outside. Or perhaps it was looking into the house, at all the people living there, observing all the things they were doing, remembering all the things that they had done. It didn't help to close the shutter. I could still see the Eye staring at me, through me.

With the Eye on me, I made a decision that I hoped would solve my moral dilemma (and keep the Eye from driving me crazy). I decided to let *Geoff* use the telescope. He seemed to have no scruples about it. If he insisted on doing it, it absolved me of guilt. Let him sit there, like Odin, and look out. I, on the other hand, the All-Mother, would look inward, in the other direction, as Millicent had asked me to do. I would find out all I could about the people living at Odin's Eye: Millicent, Lummie, Mayne Cooper, all of them.

Obviously, I'd start with Olive Plumtree.

— EIGHT

This was my second dinner at Odin's Eye, and it started out innocently with me preparing crudités for the cocktail hour. We call them raw vegetables at home, and we cook them. I was mentally coping with the very idea of eating raw squash disks when Millicent looked out the window and uttered an expletive (I repeat it in its milder form).

"Oh, *shoot!*" she cried. "Here comes Doc Thomas!"

The expletive came easily from Millicent, because of her wider worldview. It would have sounded awful coming from Mother.

"He'll invite himself to cocktails," Millicent moaned, "and then he'll stay for dinner. And for the next two hours at least, he'll pepper us with horrible details about the mortuary and grisly jokes that he's collected. I wish I hadn't called him this morning. It reminded him that there's a household of women over here," she lamented. "Oh, dear God," she added as an afterthought, "I hope Olive and Lummie don't show up."

Through the window I saw this baldheaded, elderly gentleman bounding across the grass strip.

"He's an old goat," explained Millicent. "One of the trials of the summer. He'll simply infuriate Lummie."

I could hear polite cries of surprise and invitation from the company gathered on the porch, and when I took out the platter of crudités, there he was, already stretched out in the reclining chair, holding court. He jumped to his feet when he saw me, ripped off his glasses, and gave a loud cry of rapture.

"A young thing!" he bellowed. "Where did you old girls capture this young thing?"

Probably he had more energy than he knew what to do with. I couldn't imagine my tired father leaping to his feet from a reclining chair because I happened to walk out on the porch. But then, I couldn't imagine Pop, either, insulting the other ladies and looking me up and down in a way that was a lot more objectionable than poor Nate tweaking at my elbow. You have to put up with people like Doc Thomas: I could almost hear Mother sigh, her invariable reaction to the facts of life. I was a little amused to see how unruffled the old girls, as he called them, were. All of them were used to old goats, I guess. I suppose it never occurred to him that that's what he was.

"Why didn't the cannibals boil the priest?" he inquired, laying himself down again, and managing to make the question sound ominously off-color. Everyone was apprehensive. Millicent, glancing in my direction, looked really annoyed.

"Because he was a friar," said Doc Thomas blandly. Since they had expected the worst, they were all furious at him. I heard a few faint groans, a wondering exclamation from Mayne Cooper, and a snort from Regina, who glanced at him with contempt. She could get even with him, of course, by writing him into a book.

The cocktail hour was full of insults and suggestive remarks, and when Doc Thomas didn't leave and had to be invited to supper, we gathered around the table in not the greatest of spirits. Like Millicent, I ardently hoped that Lummie and Olive wouldn't show up to fill the empty chairs, but they did.

Doc Thomas's face lit up with ominous pleasure. "Well, by God, Lummie!" he shouted in a voice that implied that Olive was a desirable woman and none of the others at the table were (I didn't count) and, at the same time, that so far as Lummie was concerned, there must have been some terrible mistake. Lummie sort of cringed, but Olive turned slightly in Doc Thomas's direction and simply looked at him.

It reminded me of Perkins, our neighbor's English setter, yapping and prancing across the garden after our cat. When she'd had enough, she'd turn and face him, and poor old Perkins would come to a screeching halt, all four paws dug into the tulip bed. Then he'd begin to study the sky and count the clouds, inching one leg backwards at a time.

There was something about Olive's look that drained all Doc Thomas's allusions to sex out of the conversation, and he began, in a most gentlemanly way, to praise the fish, which I had watched Millicent poach in wine, with bay leaves, coriander, tiny rings of onions, and a touch of tarragon.

"The fish is excellent," said Olive coolly, and there were assents of approval. "Where do you get such lovely fresh sole?" she asked Millicent.

"Geoff and I rowed over to Nate's and got it," I explained, and then remembered that Lummie might have some feelings about Nate. But he ignored the remark. And me.

"Nate's getting much worse," Doc Thomas observed. "I've been watching him. Eventually he'll have to be hospitalized, I suppose."

"He's always been a little off," Lummie snapped. "He can't be that much worse."

"Poor little Nate," said Aunt Tattie sadly, obviously thinking way back on her teaching years. "He was always at the bottom of the pecking order."

"If you think I was pecking at Nate, I beg to differ," said Lummie crossly. "I wasn't in his class. I was hardly in the same generation, in case you've forgotten." A gratuitous remark, considering Aunt Tattie's age. I think she caught the meanness of it, but she made no outward sign except a quick glance at Lummie.

"Well, *I* was in your class, Lummie," said Millicent. "And I thoroughly enjoyed pecking at you."

"I remember it well," said Lummie at once. "You still enjoy it."

It was meant to be funny, but no one laughed except for the low rumble in Olive's throat. Aunt Tattie, trained by profession when to see and when not to see, serenely ate her supper. A small silence ensued.

"My mother says you were in her homeroom at high school," I said tentatively to Olive. Olive looked startled.

"Who was your mother?" she asked, and I told her my mother's maiden name. "She'll be surprised that you're here," I added.

"She told Cicely that you hadn't been heard of since high school," Millicent put in with a short laugh. I figured I hadn't contributed a lot to the harmony of the evening—first Nate, then Olive. Lummie put his glass down with a thump.

"Olive is an expert in her field," he said indignantly to Millicent. "What do you mean, 'never heard of'? She's written the most authoritative book we have on—" But here Olive *sssted,* the faintest cat-like warning, and Lummie stopped dead in his tracks. I doubt that anyone heard the hiss but Lummie and me, for he was sitting beside her, and I directly across the table. Millicent had turned angrily away. The wariness I saw in Olive's face—was it because of Lummie's remark or because I had mentioned Mother, or both?

"Tell your mother hello when you talk to her, Cicely," Olive said, with great composure. "She was always very nice to me." My question remained unanswered.

"Quite a brouhaha in the bay this morning," observed Doc Thomas. I had watched his eyes darting from Lummie to Millicent to Olive, and I figured he hadn't missed much of the contretemps. "One of those military snafus. I understand they were bringing the working model of some military satellite to the base here. They've got some special project going this summer. Testing or something, I presume. The Moreheads up the bay fished the pilot out of the water all right, but the plane went down. It must have been important cargo, because the pilot headed right for the phone and dripped water all over the Morehead's dining room while he called the base. They apparently sent the Coast Guard and copters right out, and they've been diving all day for the damn thing."

"Did they find it?" asked Regina. I saw her round black eyes glisten.

"Ask Lummie," said Doc Thomas. "He ought to know. Secret communications are his bag, aren't they?" Lummie scowled.

"I saw you out on the pilings, Lummie," Regina said. "Did the divers find anything?"

Lummie hunched over his plate. He didn't answer, but Olive said smoothly, "It was part of our project that they were delivering to the base. They found the heavier parts of the plane, but not the model. I'm afraid it has already washed out to sea. The tidal current is terribly strong out there in the channel. It's a real loss of time, for one thing." She looked thoughtfully at Regina. "I was also watching the diving, from a yacht near the buoy," she added.

"I saw you, too," Regina said. "I've been glued to the bird glasses all day."

And with that, I thought, the mystery was blown away. Trust old Doc Thomas to know somebody who knew somebody. A plane had gone down, some equipment was lost, something Olive and Lummie were concerned about from work, and they'd both been watching. That was all. The undercurrents I'd sensed had no more meaning than the pull of the tide. I got up to clear the plates for dessert.

"Nate's upset about the thing, though," Doc Thomas said. "I went over there this afternoon, and he was pretty incoherent. He knew they were looking for something out in the bay—he'd been out there early this morning, fishing."

"As a matter of fact," said Aunt Tattie, "I dropped in to see him myself, just before supper. I was taking him some little things he needed. He's always out of socks—the salt water rots them. He was quite agitated. He kept saying over and over, "I know where it is! I know where it is!"

"Know where what is?" asked Regina.

"Why, Captain Kidd's treasure, I suppose," Aunt Tattie said. "That's what he's usually upset about. I don't know what he meant, but he kept muttering, 'The Eye will see!' "

Lummie made a gagging sound. "It had better not!" he threatened. "Any more of that spying, and someone else is going to get hurt."

I heard Olive's warning hiss, and the plate I was lifting froze in the air. I stopped breathing. Millicent turned on Olive.

"Just who are you?" she demanded. "And what exactly are you doing here?"

"It's none of your damn business what she's doing here, Millicent," Lummie shouted. "She's my guest."

Millicent winced, as if he had slapped her in the face.

"That is quite enough, Robert," said Aunt Tattie. "Haven't you done enough damage already?"

Doc Thomas brought his fist down on the table.

"How does Nate know where the treasure is?" he thundered. His face was blotched red and purple.

"He *doesn't* know where it is," Regina said coldly. "Kidd never came this far north. I have done considerable research on the matter."

I was still frozen, the plate only halfway up from the table. In the silence that followed these outbursts, we all hung suspended in space.

"Captain Kidd's treasure!" Mayne Cooper's voice floated sweetly down the table. Her eyes glowed. Mayne Cooper, I suddenly thought, up in the clouds, floating serenely above the uproar below, seeing nothing she didn't want to see. I knew what she was going to say—I mouthed it with her. "How *interesting!*"

NINE

And then civility took over. The trouble with civility is that it leaves questions dangling in the air. None of mine had been answered; they had only deepened, and new ones had added themselves to the others. I spent the rest of the dinner worried to death about the telescope hanging inside my jeans leg. I didn't know whether to be more scared of Lummie or of Olive. I like cats, but when I hear them hiss, I don't underestimate their capacities.

In the middle of the night, I woke up hearing my mother say clearly, "She was Croatian." I tried, but I couldn't figure out what was so important about that. I decided my subconscious was just working overtime, so I mentally thanked the computer person up there and went back to sleep.

The next time I saw him, I told Geoff about the dinner, but I couldn't make all the ins and outs dramatic enough, and he wasn't even faintly interested in Olive's hisses.

"Have you seen anything out on the bay?" he asked.

"I haven't looked," I answered. "Lummie said he'd . . ."

"That nerd!" Geoff exploded. "Look, Cicely, that's your *job!* If you're going to find out what's going on, you've got to keep watch."

"It's *your* job," I said. "I'm looking inward."

"I don't know what you're talking about," he said crossly. "What do you mean—*inward?*"

"I can't betray Millicent," I said. "She doesn't want the telescope back in the house."

"Well, she wants you to find out what this Olive Plumtree is up to, doesn't she?" he asked hotly. "What's the difference?"

"Your responsibility is the telescope," I said firmly. "I'm concentrating on Olive Plumtree and what she's doing here."

"I think you're nuts, Cicely," Geoff said at last, and the argument terminated on that lovely note.

Even after the Coast Guard abandoned the search for the model, Olive stayed on at Odin's Eye. Or perhaps you would say she just didn't leave. Millicent made some martyred remarks out in the kitchen, but I was beginning to understand that she was incapable of facing up to Lummie, or of breaking off with him.

It was a funny relationship, Lummie's and Olive's. They came and went together, but their conversation, though informal, didn't seem very chummy to me. Lummie often joined the group after supper, walking the shore and later reading companionably in the lamplight or listening to recordings. Olive kept to herself for the most part, and I wondered what she did with her long evenings. Millicent must have noted that Olive treated Lummie as if it were her business to tolerate him, but no more. Yet, peculiar relationship or not, they were a closed corporation. If she didn't have any other grounds for worry, Millicent certainly could have worried about the witch-like power that Olive seemed to have over him.

It seemed strange to me that the guests at Odin's Eye—and even Millicent to a certain extent—accepted and actually appeared to enjoy Olive's company. Olive liked to cook, and on evenings when they were doing something Eastern European, you'd hear them all chattering and laughing away in the kitchen. Sometimes they called me in to lend a hand, and I liked to watch Olive when she was enjoying herself like this. She looked less stealthy somehow, and she'd throw back her head and laugh in such an infectious way that I could understand why Mother had remembered her and liked her. I couldn't figure it out.

I gave the whole business less thought than I might have, because of Geoff. In spite of our argument, he came to Odin's Eye every day. First he'd check the bay with the telescope, and then he'd help me with my chores or he'd do extra things for Millicent. Then we'd take off somewhere, either in the boat, or sometimes in the family car, if he could get it. He'd just gotten his driver's license. He was a good driver and paid attention, which I remember my sister, at his age, did not. I was in the car when Winnie became so interested in watching a fender bender in the other lane that she caused one in hers, the result of which was a family discussion without civility.

One afternoon, Geoff took me off to explore the bay area. He'd lived there for a long time, and we drove on to what looked like an old Dutch windmill that was set all by itself in the middle of a wheatfield. He told me that at some centennial or other they had put sails on it. It must have been really beautiful sitting out there in the wheatfield, its white sails set against the blue sky with the sea as background. Only the bare bones of the vanes were there now, though it was still a nice picture. The mill was in the lower part. You could go inside, and we did. It was dusty, the dust undisturbed, so I gathered not many people walked all the way out there to look at it. The millstone was still in place, and I got really absorbed in the great shaft, and the gear machinery, which surprised Geoff. Did he think I wasn't capable of understanding anything more complicated than a hair dryer?

For the celebration, probably, some bags of grain had been set out there in the mill, but the field mice had long since ripped into them and carried away all of the kernels. There were barrels and boxes stowed in the dark corners under the heavy beams, and a lot of old iron. We sat for a while on an old bench that was there. Geoff moved close to me, but I thought it was neither the time nor the place, so I leaped to my feet.

Then we drove into town and finished off our afternoon at the drugstore, sitting on high stools at the counter. There were a lot of local kids hanging around, and it was fun to give them the eye. The girls, and I'm sure Geoff knew them, backed away, looking hostile and amazed, which gave me a feeling of unaccustomed power.

Another day Geoff showed up with two bicycles attached to his car. We drove to another point and then he parked near a lighthouse. We explored all over on our bicycles, discovering things you can't see from the road, though nothing we found was all that important. I guess I'll never feel better in my whole life than I did that day, on a vacation beside the sea. The sun was hot on my back, but the sea breeze slid up my shirt and cooled me off in a way that would have been impossible inland at home. I could have bicycled forever—with Geoff.

On our way back, I spotted a cemetery on one side of the road. The grass was overgrown and the headstones disappeared into the surrounding woods. I was curious, because the headstones were all alike, just small upright stone slabs.

"It's Quaker, I think," said Geoff. "The town one's down the road. I've never been in this one." I wanted to see it, so we dropped our bikes in the long grass and walked back. We prowled around, looking at the gravestones. Just the name and dates were engraved on them—no little verses or anything—and the stones were plain, without angels or decorations. I liked reading the names. I could just see LYDIA COUNTRYMAN, 1877–1930, in her gray dress with a white collar and a little cap, looking at us with disapproval as we walked idly around the graves.

We were at the far edge of the cemetery when we heard a car slow down in the road. Geoff must have been feeling like an intruder, as I was, though there really wasn't anything wrong about walking around like that, and we were in fact rather subdued by the peace and quiet of the place. But we both instinctively withdrew into the woods, out of sight.

A man got out of the car and came our way, but he turned, walked toward a little grove of trees to one side, and sat down on an old stone bench there, really hidden. Geoff and I looked at one another, but we hesitated to come crashing out of the woods—the man would wonder what we had been doing back in there, which was nothing, of course. Geoff sort of protectively put his arm around me, but I wasn't very comfortable. And then we got the shock of our lives.

A second car pulled up, and a tall woman walked directly to the stone bench. It was Olive Plumtree. She sat there talking with the man—very earnestly, if I know anything about body language. We couldn't hear them from that distance, of course. Then Olive walked quickly back to the car and after checking up and down the road, got in and drove away. In a few minutes the man did the same thing, also checking the road.

"I wonder who she really is," Geoff said when they were gone.

"I don't know," I answered, "except that she's Croatian."

Geoff glanced down at me. "You say the wierdest things, Cicely," he complained.

"Well, that's what my mother told me. She and Olive knew each other in high school," I explained. "And I know she wrote a book, because Lummie started to talk about it at dinner, and she hushed him up."

Geoff looked troubled. "I think this is serious," he said. "I ought to tell Dad about it. He doesn't trust Lummie. No one around here does. He said he'd feel a lot safer about national security if Lummie weren't working with the INT agencies."

"INT?"

"Intelligence. There's a bunch of them. SIGINT. COMINT. ELINT . . ."

"You sound like alphabet soup, Geoff," I remarked, and then thought that was a dumb thing to say.

Geoff continued patiently, as if I hadn't interrupted. "Communications surveillance. That's not for publication, though, what Dad said."

"You can't tell your father about Olive and Lummie unless you have something definite," I pointed out. "If you accuse them of spying and you can't prove it, you just leave them torn and bleeding. That's really dangerous." Geoff nodded. "Especially with Olive," I added reluctantly.

"I thought you were more scared of Lummie," Geoff said.

"I'm scared of Lummie all right," I said soberly, "but Olive is . . . well—"

"Olive hisses: Is that it?" Geoff looked down at me and laughed, but immediately became serious.

"I wonder what her book was about," he said. "That might answer some questions."

"Well, we could go to a library and find out," I suggested.

"What if the library doesn't have it?" Geoff asked. "It probably won't. Do you know if there's an index or something that lists all the books?"

"I don't know," I answered. "Probably. I'll ask Regina."

"Be careful," Geoff warned. "Ask about something else." This was good advice, and I resolved to follow it. We were back on the trail, and the nicest part was having Geoff along. Before we emerged from the woods, I thought from the way he glanced down at me he might kiss me. But he looked uncertain and didn't.

— TEN

I cornered Regina and asked her about her research into Captain Kidd. She was pleased to be asked, and I got a lot of information I didn't need, but I did find out where to look for all the books that have been published. CBI, she said. I didn't ask what the initials stood for, but I did gather we'd have to go to a central library somewhere. Geoff turned his charm on Millicent. She was delighted to have us go, she said, and we drove to the nearest big city.

I am used to libraries, and this one, though larger than the one I haunt, was characteristic. "They all *smell* alike," said Geoff.

The CBI (*Cumulative Book Index,* as I found out) was arranged by year, or groups of years, and though we went back thirty-five years for safety's sake, there was no mention of any book by Olive Plumtree. The librarian was very nice to us, which meant she looked us over, decided we knew what we were doing, and left us alone. But when we showed signs of frustrations, she came right over.

"I wonder if she wrote under a pen name?" she

suggested. This was a depressing thought, since there was obviously no way in the world of knowing what it would be. We walked slowly down the staircase and out into the sunlight, where we sat on the steps to think.

"What pen name would she possibly use? Something in Croatian, I suppose," I said darkly. "I wonder if her folks were refugees, or what? *She* looks American enough."

"There's a guy at school named Archangel," Geoff said. "That's his last name. Really!" he added, answering my look of incredulity. "The Immigration people got it all mixed up when his folks came from Italy."

"Maybe the Immigration people got Olive Plumtree all mixed up, too. It's such a kooky name," I said idly.

"I wonder what *plum* is in Croatian," said Geoff, also idly. Maybe—" but I had jumped to my feet, and was streaking, hell-bent for leather, to the reference room.

The Croatian dictionary had a word for plum, *šljiva* and also a word for the tender of plums, *šljivić,* maybe someone who would work in an orchard?

We went back upstairs, and the CBI lady was as excited as we were—librarians have the souls of detectives anyhow. She stayed right with us, and *she* was the one who squealed out loud when she found it.

> Šljivić, Olivia. *Sig Com. The growth of electronic encoding and surveillance.* American Science Press, 1977.

The librarian said *American Science* was a magazine that printed a lot of technical articles, and it also published books. We copied everything down.

"Who or what is Sig Com?" I asked, as we went back into the bright sun.

"Never heard of it," Geoff said.

"Grandpa was in the Signal Corps during the war," I observed. "He worked on a secret machine that sent out codes." Having had so little reaction earlier from Millicent when I mentioned Grandpa, I wasn't prepared for Geoff's enthusiasm. He stopped right in the middle of the sidewalk, causing annoyance and a lot of the patient exasperation reserved for teenagers.

"Is he alive?" he asked.

"Who?"

"Your grandfather!" and when I laughed, he said, "We'll call him up right now."

"I'll have to call Winnie to get the number," I said. "If I call Mom, I'll have to explain everything." Winnie was in a dither—you could hear Georgie in the background bellowing—and she didn't ask a single question.

We found out that Sig Com was an electronic code scrambler used to confound the Germans during the World War II. Grandpa was specially trained to maintain it. He said it was a complicated gadget and he still had the tools he used when he worked on it. Then he wanted to know why I was interested, and I used up all my change, and Geoff's, explaining evasively about Odin's Eye and what I was doing in New England.

When that was over, we went to a hamburger place.

"Well," said Geoff, "we know a few things we didn't know before. We know for sure that Olive's an expert in secret communications."

"I don't understand why she used the Croatian name for her book, though." I was worried. "It points right to the fact that she's doing something behind the Iron Curtain. Spies wouldn't be that dumb, would they?"

"Not that one. She even *looks* like a spy."

"Whatever a spy looks like," I pointed out. "The man she was talking to in the cemetery didn't look unusual. I didn't even know whether he was American or not. How can you tell?"

We sat there sipping our Cokes and gnawing away at our hamburgers. Even though Geoff didn't say a lot, he seemed to be getting more and more involved. I thought he looked really handsome when he was thinking hard. He didn't sweat, the way some of the football guys do in English class. I was the one who was sweating. The more I thought, the more anxious I got. My courage ebbed away, like the Coke in my plastic glass, growing weaker and more diluted until there was nothing but slush ice left in the bottom. Something—everything—warned me to stop the whole business. Right then at that moment.

Whatever we had stumbled into was real, not storybook. I was fascinated by Olive, because in her way she was the most beautiful woman I had ever seen. But I wasn't fool enough not to know that she was far smarter than anyone else at Odin's Eye, and ruthless in a way the others would never imagine. I hadn't watched cats play with mice without learning something about them.

And I was more afraid of Lummie than I wanted to admit. For if Nate feared the man of God, so did I. His threat about the Eye terrified me. I thought even Millicent had dark suspicions about Lummie, which she didn't dare confront, and that Doc Thomas, certainly Nate, and even Aunt Tattie, in spite of anything they said or didn't say, suspected him of foul play. And I thought Odin had known something, and Peter Kugle as well, and that both of them had carried the secret, probably unwillingly, to their graves.

— Eleven

I began to have nightmares.

That first night, I dreamed the Eye was looking all around the room for me, like a searchlight, poking into corners and under furniture. Even though I was trying to yell for help, and my voice would only make horrible little squeals, the Eye found me in my bed. It got bigger and bigger and more and more purple, and then Lummie was right in the middle of it. I could see him step out, and I knew he was going to kill me. Another strangled squeal woke me up, and, drenched in sweat, I lay there waiting for Pop to shout, "For goodness' sake, Cicely, wake up!" When I finally realized where I was, I understood why no one would have heard me. A nor'easter—which Millicent had said was coming, and in preparation for which we had carried in all the porch chairs—had arrived.

Up until then, a nor'easter was something I'd read about in seafaring tales—ships lost on the deep and seals that washed ashore in the storm, and then turned into human lovers or sweethearts, only to change back into seals, just as happiness seemed within their grasp. I wasn't prepared for the darkness of the nor'easter, the cold, the relentless washing of the waves, the sea spray that covered all the windows, and the general wetness that attacked my jeans hanging in the closet, my underwear and T-shirts in the dresser, the bedclothes. There was a desperate air of being shut in forever, which not even a fire in the fireplace could dispel. A nor'easter and a summer home in tandem make a perfect breeding place for trouble. I didn't know this at the time, because my chief concern was that the ocean not come any further over the seawall than it already had.

"Once I had to crawl out the kitchen window," observed Millicent with equanimity. "During a hurricane. The sea washed right underneath the house."

Hurricanes are one up from nor'easters, but I did check the window in the kitchen.

"Just in case we have to leave in a hurry and we can't get the door unlocked," I explained to Geoff, who had blown in with a load of wood.

At first it was pretty lively at Odin's Eye. We all played games, and there was a lot of jollity, as if Aunt Tattie had waited all her life to play a wild round of Ping-Pong on the dining room table or Regina to cavort about on the rug, swatting croquet balls through little wickets. But the storm continued without any letup, and by afternoon, Regina had vanished into her room in the right wing—I could hear her typewriter banging away. Aunt Tattie retired for a small nap. The others peeled off, one by one, except for Mayne Cooper, who was writing letters on a lapboard, apparently oblivious to the storm.

She looked lavendary-and-old-lace sitting there in the lamplight, the gale howling around her. It struck me suddenly how fond I had become of the four ladies. They were all interesting in their own right, and they knew so much and had so much assurance and dignity in handling their lives. I'd often thought if anything happened to Pop, Mother would have an awful time adjusting to the world, like a nun going over the wall, if that's the right expression. Not that she wasn't competent, but she hadn't seen much beyond our little town.

That reminded me that Mother had worried because Millicent's friends "saw things differently from us," and as I watched Mayne Cooper, I wondered what Mother really meant. It seemed to me that the only difference between them and us was that Millicent and Millicent's friends were handling life without men telling them what to do all the time, or expecting to have Aunt Tatties around to go out and buy them new socks because their old ones had holes in them.

I got awfully mad at men in general, thinking about the ladies. I was still cross about my nightmare, Lummie pinning me down like that. I thought maybe it was about time that All-Mothers *did* take over the Eye business and run things in their own way for a change. It occurred to me that this was precisely what Mother was afraid of, that she didn't at all like the idea of women running things, probably because Pop didn't.

At any rate, this revelation made me simply furious at Geoff, though he was just sitting there at an old piano that must have been in the cottage for years and that Millicent kept reasonably in tune for her guests. I glared at him, he looked so satisfied with himself and life.

Then he patted the other half of the piano bench in a way that was partly command and partly invitation, and smiled his nice slow smile, and it was all so irresistible that I got right up and sat down beside him at the piano.

"Can you scat?" I asked.

"Sure can," he said cheerfully. So we scatted, which means you sing tone syllables without moving your teeth—choirs always have to do it to improve their voices and they usually end up hating Fred Waring, who formalized it for schools, but we didn't hate it this time. Geoff turned out to be pretty good. He was going to school at one of those New England academies where they seem to teach a lot of extra things, and he sang in the school choir. He scatted a lot better than I did.

Then we got to splicing. I played the melody in one time pattern and he interwove the bass in another. We were pretty absorbed—splicing is hard to do—and when we got to the end, more or less together, I heard a voice say, "Very nice."

I hadn't seen Olive come in, but there she was, tucked rather spookily into a corner under the stairs. The shadows accentuated the lines of her face and made the high cheekbones even more prominent. She had just been sitting there, waiting out the storm, not reading or anything. It made me feel a little jumpy, knowing she had been watching us, and also a little sad, because she did look lonely, off in the corner there, while Geoff and I had been having so much fun together on the piano bench.

And it *had* been fun. In an intellectual sort of way. I'd been so absorbed in the music that I hadn't even thought about the two of us sitting close together on the bench, our hands and arms entwined. I glanced at Geoff, and he gave me sort of a funny look. Something was wrong. I couldn't imagine any of the girls at school sitting there like that and not squealing in ecstasy as they told about it next day in front of their lockers at school. I hadn't felt one tiny little bit of ecstasy: It wasn't very normal of me.

"Time for tea!" called Mayne Cooper in a tinkly voice.

It reminded me of one of those bells they used to ring for the servants, and I got up hastily from the piano bench. At that moment Millicent appeared with a big tray.

Tea is a serious business in a place like Odin's Eye, and especially in the middle of a nor'easter. Both Geoff and I trotted back and forth carrying plates of sandwiches and lemons stuck through with cloves. I felt guilty that Millicent had been doing all that work while Geoff and I were fooling around at the piano, but she just said with a pleasant smile, "No—no—that's perfectly all right, Cicely."

Mayne Cooper had launched into one of her travelogues again. She was in Yugoslavia this time, with Ernestine.

"Who's Ernestine? Her sister?" I asked Millicent out in the kitchen.

"No," said Millicent. "A friend. They've lived together for years. They're inseparable, both travelers. But somebody told them they ought to spend part of their life apart, for their mental health or something, and they assiduously do it, though it makes both of them perfectly miserable."

I laughed.

"Mayne's off in the ether," Millicent commented. "She's a little woolly sometimes. Ernestine keeps her grounded."

When I got back with a new plate of cookies and tea cakes, Miss Cooper was still talking about Yugoslavia.

"We were arrested!" she said with a merry laugh. "Ernestine and I went out for an evening walk, and we got into some sort of restricted area. A guard came rushing out, and we had to go to the police station."

"*Mayne!!*" shrieked everyone in horror. But Miss Cooper merely opened her eyes wide in innocence and said, "Oh, we were scared to death!" Suddenly she stopped talking.

"Olive," she said after a moment, in a wondering tone, "I know now where I saw you."

"If you have seen me before, Miss Cooper, I can

assure you it was not in Yugoslavia." I have never heard an icier voice. And I don't know how Olive managed in a single sentence to make Mayne Cooper sound like an addled old fool, but she did.

"Oh, I beg your pardon," Mayne said in confusion, though it was an honest mistake, if it was a mistake at all, and I felt sorry for her. I glanced at Olive.

She had sunk back so far into the shadows that I could scarcely see her. She turned to Lummie, who was sitting nearby, and spoke to him in a low voice. A strange thing happened.

Lummie, as easily as you turn on a tap in the sink, began to exude charm and vitality. He took charge of the conversation, his face softened with humor, and he began to pun, so outrageously that even I had to laugh. He was nice to Millicent, too, and she bloomed right before our eyes. Geoff looked completely thunderstruck. I gathered this was a Lummie he hadn't expected. And it was certainly one that explained a lot more about Millicent, why there had been a relationship in the first place, why it refused to die. I couldn't believe what I was seeing and hearing. Everyone forgot about Yugoslavia.

I glanced once more at Olive, and I looked hastily away. I didn't want her to catch me watching her, because I didn't want the look that she was directing at Mayne Cooper to turn on me.

The event of the next day was no surprise to me. The storm was still with us, and I had begun to think the howling and pounding would never stop. We were all getting cabin-fever, so Millicent took Regina, Aunt Tattie, and me out into the storm to go shopping. Mayne Cooper, after a lot of indecisive debate with herself, decided to stay home and write to Ernestine.

When we got back, we found the garden entrance to her room open. The room was a shambles of open drawers, a closet door flung wide, though a fragrance of lilac wafted out to us as we stood huddled in the hallway. But Mayne Cooper had disappeared.

— TWELVE

"Shouldn't we call the police?" I asked in panic. I was thinking of Peter Kugle, how he was shot, how his body was found bloated and water-soaked down on the shore. My stomach was in knots. Poor, dear Mayne Cooper!

"Well, her car's gone," Regina pointed out in her practical, rather sardonic voice. "Whatever disaster has overtaken her, at least she was able to drive."

"I wonder if something happened to her friend," Millicent said in distress. "Oh, dear."

"She'll telephone," Aunt Tattie assured us. "But I wonder why she didn't leave a note. It's not like her to cause us worry."

But that's what she was doing, all right. Among my private worries was how much I should or should not say. How much did I really know? How much did I want Olive or Lummie to know about me and my suspicions? Answer: not one thing.

In an atmosphere of British stiff upper lip, Regina set herself to preparing a stir-fry for dinner, and I was conscripted into the operation as general chopper and peeler. I was glad of the activity because we were all waiting for the telephone to ring. I wanted to shake that black old thing, it sat there on the bookshelf so unfeeling and so silent.

Olive and Lummie drove in just before dinner. They professed such concern for Mayne Cooper that I had to conclude that either I was horribly mistaken in my suspicions, or else the two of them were cold-bloodedly clever. I thought the latter, but my role was to chop carrots and shut up. I did both of these things.

At dinner the telephone finally rang, and Millicent nearly upset the table in her haste to answer it. We all sat there tingling with curiosity as she relayed Mayne Cooper's conversation to us, repeating each sentence that she heard, like an old-fashioned preacher lining out a hymn.

> The most fantastic thing! We are absolutely dumbfounded! Why, we just can't *understand* . . .

Millicent inserted small interruptions from time to time:

> MILLICENT: Understand *what,* Mayne? What on earth happened to you?
> MAYNE: Just after you left for the store, the telephone rang, and this *strange* voice—
> MILLICENT: Had you ever heard it before?

MAYNE: Why no, never . . . it was a *man's* voice. . . . He said that Ernestine had had an accident and I was to come home immediately. . . . yes. . . . I had a *terrible* trip home!

MILLICENT: We were frightened when we saw your empty room. . . . Mayne, what has happened to Ernestine?

MAYNE: Oh dear, I do hope I didn't leave my room in a mess . . . no? Oh, I am so relieved. . . .

MILLICENT: Mayne, *what happened to Ernestine!* Is she all right?

MAYNE: Ernestine? Why, she was perfectly all right! She met me at the door! No, nothing had happened to her at all . . . some mistake . . . some other poor soul . . . oh, dear no, I couldn't leave Ernestine now. I'd worry every single minute . . . but isn't that the most. . . .

It was indeed the most, I thought indignantly. What if something had happened to Mayne on her wild terrible trip home? Olive's little purrs of condolence didn't do one thing to help matters. Everything shows on my face; I was glad that I had plates to clear away and general bustle to cover up with while the exclamations and the purrs went on and on. Cats, Mother says, show no guilt because they are amoral. But sometimes cats are downright wicked, and if you catch them in the act, you're within your rights to swat them one. I wanted to swat Olive.

Not having Mayne Cooper with us made for a jagged table conversation. Various topics were tried out: None succeeded. After the coffee was poured into Millicent's beautiful blue cups, which her seafaring ancestors had brought from China, we all sat around the table without saying much of anything. It seemed to me that there were plenty of dark thoughts brewing, though maybe mine were the blackest. Suddenly I heard the sound of breaking brush, with accompanying little hoots and labored breathing, and through the bushes that surrounded the house charged old Doc Thomas. He galloped across the lawn, up the porch steps, and burst into the dining room.

"Nate's found Captain Kidd's treasure!" he bellowed.

Lummie sort of choked, and all eyes turned on him.

"Damn! Damn! Damn!" he said under his breath, and emphasized it with his clenched fists. Olive didn't even move. I thought immediately of the silent freezing of a cat when it is threatened or catches sight of its prey—how with no perceptible movement, it lowers itself close to the ground.

I was really puzzled. Up until now, most of my researches into Olive and Lummie had had a certain logic, at least, if not illumination. Each little bit of the enemy agent plot fit into something else. But what

Nate and Captain Kidd had to do with the business, I couldn't imagine. When the group moved to the porch, I stashed plates into the dishwasher in a hurry because I assumed the conversation was continuing, and I didn't want to miss any more of it than I had to. All those dear little coffee cups had to be washed by hand, and though I usually enjoyed doing it, tonight they were a big headache.

It took me a while to pick up the threads of the conversation. Nate, it seems, had hidden the treasure; Doc Thomas hadn't actually seen it. No one knew where he'd found it either. He wouldn't tell.

"He's got it, all right," stated Doc Thomas.

"I don't believe it," Regina said, shaking her head. "Not possible. I tell you, Kidd was never in these parts."

"Aha!" shouted Doc Thomas, and I thought Regina, smart as she was, had met her match. With a great display of drama, he drew a small gold coin out of his sweater pocket and archly presented it to Regina on the back of his hand. "What do you think of this? I found it in my garden. Coins of the realm don't grow in cucumber beds, now do they, *Ms.* Peppers?"

Regina was divorced; everyone called her Mrs. Peppers, her choice, and the *Ms.*, the way Doc Thomas said it, was designed to cause a reaction, and not a nice one either. After this embarrassing business, Lummie got up from his chair muttering, "Bloody old fool," and strode off to his room. Olive, as usual, had not joined the group after supper, and this left only a small audience for old Doc Thomas. Lummie's words had taken some of the bluster out of him. He rather unobstrusively put the coin back in his sweater and, after a little hemming and hawing, left. He looked lonely, as Olive so often did, and I thought I was getting pretty soupy to feel sorry for all the villains in the piece.

"Where'd he get the coin, do you suppose?" Regina asked when he was gone. She was angry and made no attempt to hide the fact.

"Oh, he found it in the cucumber patch all right." Millicent laughed, but without mirth. "Peter Kugle planted it one summer when I was here. Odin and he had a wonderful time with the Eye, watching Nate and Doc digging all over the place. Peter did it to tease the two of them, and probably to amuse Odin, though I never thought it was funny."

"Why didn't you tell them it was a hoax?" Aunt Tattie asked. "Peter was so cruel to poor Nate."

"And cross Grandfather?" Millicent replied.

"I'll tell him," Regina said. "I don't mind at all. In fact, it would give me pleasure."

My grandmother has an ancient set of books called *The Bookhouse,* and over the years I've read them cover to cover. There's a poem in one about finding Spanish gold, and I couldn't read it—I couldn't even see the picture—without this awful longing. I was the wrong century and the wrong sex, but I couldn't help it: "We're off to seek for Spanish gold across the Spanish Main" . . . it gave me a shivery feeling just thinking about it.

"Don't tell him, Regina," I begged.

"Why ever not?" Regina asked sharply. "He needs putting down a peg or two. Along with a few other males I could mention, my dear departed being one."

I guess I shouldn't have been startled at the bitterness of Regina's response. I was out of my depth completely, and I didn't answer.

"Doc's a romantic at heart," Aunt Tattie said after a moment. "He's just not very good at it. Cicely's probably right. It's better to leave him with a few dreams, even if it's fool's gold."

"Ha!" Regina snorted. I could see that she was blind to any suggestion that Doc had a softer side. I couldn't blame her, I must say. I didn't like him either.

"No one's going to listen to him anyway," Millicent observed. "The neighbors have heard this Captain Kidd business before. About once a year, in fact. No one will pay the least attention to Nate *or* to Doc Thomas."

"Then why was Lummie . . ." I started to say, but the DON'T placard rose up suddenly in front of me and I swallowed my words midway. No wonder Sherlock Holmes was a great success. He played the violin instead of yakking.

A few days later, when I was setting the table in the dining room, Doc Thomas strode up on the porch where Lummie was sitting alone. The two had a terrible row. Lummie, Doc Thomas said, had visited Nate and scared him to death. Now Nate was cowering in his house and wouldn't come out. In a fury, Doc

Thomas told Lummie to keep the hell away. Lummie picked up a magazine, but you could see him smoldering behind it. After a lot of harrumphing, Doc Thomas strode off again.

Aunt Tattie went over to Nate's the next day. All Doc Thomas had said was true, and she couldn't do anything with Nate. He wouldn't eat, she said, and I could see how worried she was.

And then in another few days Doc Thomas came back again. He walked up on our porch, his puppy ebullience gone. He looked really old as he stood there, his hand on the pillar.

"Nate has been hospitalized," he told us. "The welfare people came and got him. And even though you may think I did it because of the treasure, I want you to know I am *not* responsible for his being taken away like this. I swear to God that *I* did not turn him over to the authorities."

— THIRTEEN

Doc Thomas's red alert over the treasure didn't rouse the neighborhood, but news of Nate's hospitalization did. People thought it was a pity and a shame, even though they admitted Nate was getting more and more out of touch with things. Aunt Tattie voiced her concern about the shock he seemed to be in.

"He's been terribly frightened," she insisted, with a meaningful glance at Lummie.

There was also concern about Nate's house and the belongings inside it, for he had no heirs and apparently no real relatives at all. Doc Thomas stepped in and assumed control, and everyone, according to Geoff, was relieved that he had done so. No one knew whether Nate's confinement was permanent or not. An empty house was a target for vandalism, though Doc explained to us that there was little of value there except Peter Kugle's books and whatever price one would put on the paintings. It was not my business, but I hoped that the gentle old man would be able to come home.

Aunt Tattie decided to visit Nate in the county facility, and I went with her to keep her company. In spite of her age, she still drove, a sedate old Buick, though she avoided freeways and city centers. Actually I felt safer with Aunt Tattie than I did with Millicent. It was a pretty drive though the countryside, but it ended up dismally in the hospital, which, though brave in geraniums and chintz, could hardly conceal the dreariness of its purpose. I stayed downstairs in one of the parlors while the nurse took Aunt Tattie off to see Nate. Then the telephone rang at the reception desk and someone called, "Is there a Cicely Barrows here?"

I jumped up, and the lady at the desk said with sort of a wondering look, "Mr. Kugle wants to see you. Go down the hall and take the elevator to the third floor. Or you can walk up." I walked up, not very happily, because the place was drearier even than the usual hospital and smelled miserably of food. Even so, I'd have done whatever I could for Nate.

There was not very much that we could do. Nate was lying there in bed, so white and frail that I wondered at first if he were still alive. Aunt Tattie said he'd asked for me, not by my name, but as the Millicent who liked his paintings. By the time I got there, though, he'd forgotten about it, because his face was empty and his eyes looked in on nothing at all. Aunt Tattie was really kind to him, and I tried to copy her. Most of the time he didn't answer either of us, or if he did, you couldn't understand him, but once he said something rather clearly about drawing a picture. And then he said, "You deserve it, Millicent," and he pulled himself up and began groping around on the little table beside him as if he were looking for something.

Suddenly he started yelling about the man of God. Aunt Tattie tried to hush him, but he clutched his throat in the most awful way, his thumbs in front as if he were being strangled. A couple of attendants came hurrying in.

"Better leave, ma'am," one of them said to Aunt Tattie, and we did, though we could hear Nate's despairing yells about Lummie all the way down the hall.

Aunt Tattie was clearly upset by the whole incident. When we got into the car, we just sat for a while. Her old hands trembled on the wheel.

"I don't understand it, Cicely," she said. "I just don't understand this thing at all." At last she turned the key in the ignition, and we backed out of the parking space. She hardly spoke all the way home. I kept thinking of that poor old man clutching at his throat, and I was scared to the soles of my feet.

"I think Nate will not return," said Aunt Tattie sadly at dinner that night. "He's in very frail health and the nurses there think he will not last long."

"But he was fishing until just a short time ago," Millicent argued.

"He's suffered a shock, they think," said Aunt Tattie. "He may have had a stroke or heart attack." She put down her fork. "I believe," she said quietly, "that he has been almost frightened to death."

"Damn Thomas!" cried Lummie with great vehemence. No one responded, so I don't know what they were thinking, whether it was what I was thinking. Olive showed no emotion at all. But when I cleared the dishes after supper, I noted that Lummie's dessert was not touched, and I remembered that Millicent had said once that he would perjure his soul for chocolate.

Two nights later Nate's house was vandalized. Doc Thomas, who came to tell us the news, appeared to be simply furious. He swore a lot as he told us about it. Nothing had been taken, he said—there was nothing there *to* take—but the place was pulled to pieces. Chunks out of the wall and even the floor.

"I presume, since teenagers rarely tear up the floor looking for stereos, that the vandals were after treasure," Regina said frostily. Doc Thomas started and looked sort of sick.

"Was the fireplace also torn apart?" Lummie inquired in an insinuating, yet almost triumphant way, as if at last he had his revenge after years of insults at the hands of Doc Thomas. Doc Thomas turned absolutely white, and he left without another word. After that he stopped coming over to Odin's Eye. The police arrived and had Nate's house boarded up. Geoff told me about it, and we went over to look. It's really sad to close up somebody's life like that.

It was my job to do up the bedrooms at Odin's Eye, and I was always amused by the wastebaskets. What people throw away is indicative of character. I had to empty Regina's almost daily, and I thought that some days things must have gone badly for her writing, because the pieces of manuscript were either shredded, or twisted into tortured shapes. Mayne Cooper's basket had always wafted perfume as I carried it out, and I wondered what the skunks who came to the back porch in the evenings thought about this fragrant rival in the trash bin.

A few days after Nate's house had been vandalized, I was at my cleaning chore. When Regina had accused, or almost accused, Doc Thomas of digging for Kidd's treasure inside the house, I was rather shaken. I had trusted her intelligence. But then I began to wonder if her hatred of Doc and men in general hadn't blinded her to other possibilities. I was almost sure the culprits were Lummie and Olive, and that they were also looking for the treasure, though what it had to do with spying I couldn't figure out at all.

I always kept my eyes well open when I did up Lummie's room. I didn't really expect to find a pickax or a crowbar stashed away in his closet, and I didn't. His long row of beautiful pastel shirts hung there, and all those summer suits and blazers. They were really expensive, as I knew from the labels. Lummie wasn't exactly fastidious about his room, and I always had to hang up things that were left lying around.

There are some people who can live in straitened circumstances the way Lummie did when he was young, and it doesn't bother them one way or another. Newton (my brother) is like that, except for his stereo equipment. But Lummie's outfits were always perfectly coordinated right to his matching neckties, and to his gorgeous BMW parked outside. I couldn't help but think he must have suffered agonies as a young person without funds, and I thought he would have died now rather than not be able to satisfy his taste for elegance. I supposed he could buy all these things because he didn't have any responsibilities other than himself. Pop also works for the government, and he has exactly one summer jacket, which doesn't coordinate with anything; all he asks is that it keep a low profile. But Lummie's outfits were almost the first thing you noticed about him.

I particularly watched Lummie's wastebasket. Olive never threw anything away but cigarette wrappers and once a toothpaste box, but Lummie's was always full of papers. I didn't exactly root around in the baskets, but I thought there was nothing wrong in pouring the contents of the basket slowly into the trash bin. It seemed to me any good detective would have done the same.

This day a fragment of paper did catch my eye. It was just plain white paper, but it had typed on it: *mentally conf . . .*

mentally conf! My knees buckled, even though it was exactly what I was looking for. I put the fragment carefully in my jeans pocket, and then I didn't know what to do about it.

What I did about it was a huge mistake, probably the most awful blunder of my life, and it was because of my conscience. If it were left to conscience to do the work of the world, we'd be in sad trouble. You have to attach common sense to conscience. Conscientious people like me have to keep remembering that. Particularly if their forte is detection.

What I did was tell Millicent all about my suspicions, including Lummie not eating his chocolate pudding. I even showed her the scrap of paper that I had found.

If I expected her to confront Lummie, I had that all wrong.

"In the first place," Millicent said severely, "we don't rifle through people's wastebaskets. And in the second place, if you think for a moment that Lummie was involved in this miserable business with Nate, you are greatly mistaken. He knows as well as I do that Nate is harmless. You heard Lummie tell off Doc Thomas at dinner." And it's true, he had.

But what I should also have remembered is that Millicent was unwilling, or unable, to face up to Lummie, that she kept excusing him. The problem was that I hadn't been smart enough to understand that she had never, in her own mind, broken with Lummie, and now that he had shown up again, she found herself right back in the old relationship. By the time I had figured this out, the damage was done. Because Millicent showed the piece of paper to Lummie when he and Olive came in, and asked him what it was all about. He managed to look baffled.

"You were talking about mental confusion in that

long memo you wrote to your boss, Lummie," Olive said, and his face cleared. "That's right, I did," he said.

Then his face darkened—I could actually see it.

"Are you given to searching through wastebaskets, Millicent?" he asked viciously.

Millicent had always been very nice to me, and my conscience started right in to hurt.

"I found it," I said.

And so I alerted both Olive and Lummie to the fact that I had been looking.

I hated to tell Geoff about it, how dumb I had been, but in the end I had to.

— Fourteen

"Gosh, Cicely," said Geoff in disgust. "That was really stupid."

That's probably what Adam told Eve, and I bet she was just as mad as I was. It's absolutely inexcusable to agree with someone who has just confessed to being not too bright about something. Especially if you are a girl who's been dumb, and the boy facing you is really smug, even if he is right. You get so mad you go straight back to Adam and Eve. You want to take that rib and give him a good whack with it.

"You played right into their hands," Geoff said. "Just like a woman!" And that did it.

We were sitting in front of Odin's Eye, upstairs in my "studio," and talking in low tones because only floorboards separated us from the living room, and they were full of knotholes that allowed you to see directly down. I'd often had to resist the temptation to pelt the downstairs company with mothballs, and Geoff almost didn't when I pointed out the possibilities. Today, because we had to talk, we had taken care to see that no one was within hearing range, though we still, out of habit, sort of mumbled to each other.

"I don't suppose you've ever done anything dumb in your life," I suggested in a little less than *sotto voce.* It's not easy to fight in hushed tones.

"Not that dumb," said Geoff earnestly.

"I suppose telling your father what you saw in your brother's Coast Guard boat that time was really intelligent." The end result of that incident had been a long lecture from his father on the ethics of spying, and a near miss on the use of the boat. I brought this up with all the delicacy of a karate chop.

"Thanks a lot," he said bitterly. "You sure know how to rub it in."

"Well, what do you think you were doing to me just now?" I was really mad, not just about me, but about the sexes and how it never penetrates that we have a right to say things back once in a while, even if it does destroy the male ego. I noticed that the flush on Geoff's face ran way up into his blond hair, but I didn't really care.

"It doesn't make any difference anyhow what you said or didn't say," Geoff shouted in a muffled voice. "You're not helping this spy business anyway. Look at the telescope. What's the point of it if you don't use it? You'd be watching to see what's going on in the bay if you weren't such a wimp about it."

"Well, you keep saying nothing's going on in the bay anyhow!" I muffled back. "At least *I'm* finding out something about the people in Odin's Eye. You have helped—some," I amended in a gracious tone.

"What good does it do to find out what kind of people they are if you don't know what they're doing?" Geoff asked, his voice rising in spite of the muffle. "If there's anything going on, it would be after dark. *You* have to do that. Unless you expect me to come up and spend the night with you, and I don't suppose you have that in mind," he added sarcastically. I ignored this.

"The trouble with Odin and the trouble with you," I said hotly, "is that you're so involved with that crazy telescope and the great feeling of power you get from spying on everyone in the bay, that you don't see what's going on with the people right around you. You don't even care *why* they're acting the way they do. *That's* the way you solve crimes: You have to figure out motives and things, not sit glued to a crazy spyglass watching a lot of boats!"

"Yeah," said Geoff, "and while you're analyzing all those people, all hell's breaking loose outside. Odin may have got himself and Peter Kugle killed in the end, but at least he must have discovered something."

"So what came of it?" I asked. Geoff didn't answer, and I didn't know whether it was because there wasn't an answer or because he'd given up on me. We were both kind of quiet, stewing I guess. Maybe he wasn't any happier fighting with me than I was with him.

"Millicent says her grandfather was a tyrant," I said. I don't know why it came out sounding as if I were accusing the whole male sex, but it did.

"Millicent doesn't know anything about men," Geoff grunted. "None of them do." Meaning my favorite ladies.

"They get along pretty well without men," I shot back. "They manage perfectly well without them."

"You're just like them," said Geoff, and then he bit his lip as if that had come out without his wanting it to. But it was too late.

"Maybe you'd better explain," I suggested, lying in wait.

"You never let me anywhere near you," Geoff complained. "You sit and read all the time."

"I only did that once!" I pointed out.

"We sat all afternoon together on that damn piano bench, and you didn't feel a thing!"

It was my turn to bite my lip.

We went downstairs, both unhappy. Geoff had to go home, and we walked out through the kitchen. Regina and Millicent were cubing some meat, Aunt Tattie was washing vegetables in the sink, and Olive was rolling out noodles on the old deal table, all of them chatting away like mad.

I guess Geoff and I didn't look all that cheery when we came in, because the conversation petered out, in a questioning sort of way.

"Well, we'll see you Friday, Geoff, then," said Millicent kindly. Geoff lifted his jacket off the pegs beside the door.

"Not in the afternoon, I guess," he said. "That's the night of the yacht club dance, and I have to get ready."

I couldn't believe it! There was really a silence then, and I felt as if Geoff had kicked me in the stomach. I'd been going with him all summer, hadn't I? He flushed to the top of his hair, with all those accusing eyes on him.

"Well, gee whiz, Cicely," he stammered. "I didn't think you'd be interested."

I saw red blotches in front of me. I picked the wooden spoon right out of Olive's noodle bowl and gave Geoff a clout across the chest.

And then, all those ladies at Odin's Eye, who, I bet, at some time or other had been hurt by men and who, you would think, would rejoice in the retribution meted out to Geoff at that moment, cried in unison, but on every note of the scale,

"CICELY!"

— FIFTEEN

I guessed I'd never see Geoff again. He bolted out the back door, and I raced through the dining room and porch, across the lawn to the seawall. I ran along the wall to the first place where I could jump down and stood there on the gravelly beach, facing the bay, out of sight of the house.

Geoff had hurt me, and I'd hurt him right back. We were about equal on that, and I supposed we'd both survive. I felt terrible about the people at Odin's Eye, though. I knew I'd thrown them all off balance and uncovered a part of them that neither I nor anyone else had any business seeing, a part they had probably never even shown to one another. I was unhappy about that. Also I thought of Mother and how exasperated she'd be with me. Sympathetic, too, of course, but she'd have stuck in some pithy remarks along with the condolences. The third time around, parents get hardboiled about teenagers. Mostly, right then, though, I thought about me. Pretty soon I couldn't see the bay anymore.

All your childhood you're surrounded by caring people—teachers who comfort you, and best friends and chums who stick up for you. When you're little, your parents are ready to engulf you in love and fight everyone on the block in your cause. But the very minute you hit the teens, you're alone. All the kids have their own problems, and your parents don't think you ought to have any and get mad if you do. The teachers, the young ones at least, are busy all the time, and can't stay after school for a single extra minute. There *are* some nice teachers, though, and I could just hear Miss Davis saying, "Cicely, don't take it so hard. There will be other boys, you know." But she was a million miles away, and anyhow, I wanted Geoff. All I could do was stand there and let life bat me around. I thought it was taking some pretty hard swipes. I *hated* Cicely Barrows, and I figured every single person who knew her did, too.

I began to smell cigarette smoke, so I mopped away at my eyes. Olive Plumtree came around the corner of the seawall—the wall made an L up to the house, and she must have slipped around the end and walked all the way down from the kitchen on the seaward side, where no one would see her. She lounged up against the wall, smoking and looking out to sea. She glanced down at me once—she was really tall—but she didn't seem to be in a hurry to say anything.

I never knew about Olive. Sometimes I felt sorry for her; other times I downright hated her, like the time Mayne Cooper disappeared. Mostly, not knowing who or what she was, and scared about my efforts to find out, I tried to stay out of her way. But right then I didn't care if she *was* a spy, I was so glad to have someone, anyone, standing there.

"There are almost always two sides to a problem, Cicely," Olive said at last, and quite gently. I was used to Mother's tart remarks, and Olive's kindness was so unexpected that I gulped several times before I could answer. It was occuring to me that All-Mothers are just as likely as All-Fathers to have only one eye, and that this fact, rather than the sex of either, was at the root of a lot of difficulties, mine included.

"Odin should have had two eyes like everybody else," I blurted out. I heard Olive's strange, amused chuckle.

"Men have needs, you know," Olive commented quietly. "I wish I'd understood my husband better. He was in the Air Force and stationed in out-of-the-way places. I was simply unaware of the pressures he was under, and we were divorced. He died several years ago."

She puffed a few more times on her cigarette, and then she walked back to the house, her footsteps crunching evenly on the stones as she went.

I wondered at first if Olive had heard Geoff and me fighting upstairs; she might have, but I knew that from the kitchen, she couldn't have made out what we were saying. Then I thought maybe she'd been watching me do all the wrong things with Geoff. Whatever it was, she'd been awfully nice to me just now, and I remembered she'd used those exact words once about Mother.

It's not easy to reach out to people in trouble. Nine

times out of ten you say exactly the wrong thing, and then the other person has the extra burden of forgiving you. But Olive had said all the right things. I began to wonder if Millicent was wrong about her, and if Geoff and I were mistaken as well.

I had had no idea that she'd ever been married. I wondered why she went back to her maiden name—even Regina, with all her bitterness, had not done that. I wondered if she had ever taken her husband's name in the first place. Or if she used this name professionally. And then I remembered that her profession was a spy. At least Geoff and I thought so. But I still thought she'd been really nice to me. After a while, I went back to the kitchen.

"Geoff richly deserved what he got, in my judgment," Millicent said as she assembled the salad. I couldn't help thinking that Lummie might have benefited from a whack or two on his chest, and I wondered if she'd ever considered it.

Regina, at supper, and out of nowhere, made some salty remarks about life being a compromise. While this was kindly meant, her occasional observations about the divorced Mr. Peppers had never indicated to me that she'd been awfully handy in her use of compromise, and anyhow I couldn't see how a yacht club dance could be compromised. You either went or you didn't.

Aunt Tattie didn't say anything at all to me at supper, but afterward she conspired to be sitting all alone on the porch while everyone else from Odin's Eye, even

Olive for once, went off on an evening beach walk. They usually came back with pieces of vegetation, or fragments of rock, or arcane bits thrown up by the tide. Sometimes they'd all be excited about a birdcall or some wanderer they'd seen flying past. They were the first to discover that an osprey had built its nest on the pilings, and I believe they knew about the eggs even before the mister. I found Aunt Tattie on the porch when I had finished the dinner dishes.

She glanced up from her handiwork, where she seemed to be counting knots. "Odin was a fine man," she said calmly, ignoring the fact that she'd plunged right into the middle of her thoughts. "I liked him." This really rocked me.

"But Millicent said he was a tyrant," I ventured.

"Odin did not believe that Millicent's engagement to Lummie was appropriate, and I am sure she never forgave him for it. I have wondered if he tried to force Lummie to break it up and if that was the cause of the fight that last day of Odin's life. Lummie did break off with Millicent almost immediately, of course. She was not there at the time of Odin's death, so no one will ever know exactly what was said. Unless Lummie should choose to talk about it, which is unlikely, to say the least."

"Did Lummie know something about Peter Kugle's murder?" I asked. Aunt Tattie's fingers began to work overtime, though she showed no other emotion.

"Lummie was completely cleared of the matter, and we are not to question the decision," she said severely.

She tatted a mile a minute for a while and then surprised me by laying the lace down on the table. I knew that we had got to the nitty-gritty.

"When Lummie's father was lost at sea, he left the mother and the little boy in great need. Odin assumed responsibility for them, and virtually raised Lummie. In the military tradition of course: It was all he knew. Lummie never conformed, and he hated the charity. He was not a pleasant little boy," she added, "though I often used to feel almost as sorry for him as I had earlier for Nate. Both were dominated by father figures, and Lummie had Millicent to boot. She bossed him around unmercifully."

I must have looked my question.

"Millicent was a headstrong girl from the beginning. She was at constant loggerheads with her grandfather, though he adored her."

"But what really happened?" I asked.

This question obviously bothered Aunt Tattie—I presume she had asked it of herself many times over the years. She reached down into her sweater pocket and brought up a little flowered pillbox.

"Would you mind bringing me a glass of water, Cicely? I always choke on these things." I must have looked my alarm, for she added, "Not to worry, dear. They just pep up the old ticker a little."

When I brought the glass back to the porch, I stopped for a moment in the doorway. The sunset afterglow reflected back onto the porch, and Aunt Tattie looked quite lovely sitting there. She hated the morning glare, and usually spent the early hours inside —she said that the strong light made her feel ancient, that the sunrise was for the young. But I thought even the sunset colors at their peak would have been too vibrant for her. The mauves and soft rose of this fading sky were exactly right, and I wondered if even in her youth she had ever been as beautiful as she was right then.

After she had swallowed the little tablet, she closed the box and sat for a few minutes thinking.

"Lummie was very bright, head and shoulders above the others at school," she said carefully. "I suspected—I *knew*—that he was at the bottom of a great deal of mischief, but not once did I ever catch him at it. When he grew up, he had some brushes with the law—he was frantic for money of course. Odin became increasingly impatient with him, though he saw him through college and even got him established in his career. Odin was a man of his word, and he seems to have made promises to Lummie's mother before she died."

"I still don't understand," I pleaded. Aunt Tattie looked even more worried, but continued the story.

"After the war, Odin was phased out of the Navy. Many older men were, but he took it personally and vowed his revenge. After his stroke, he and Peter Kugle contrived that silly Eye."

I nodded. Silly, though, was hardly the word for it. Evil, I thought. Aunt Tattie's next statement astounded me.

"It was a sad time for all of us, his family as well. Odin

had many friends, but he wouldn't allow any of us to see him so crippled. Only Millicent's mother, until she died, Peter, and the housekeeper. Not even Millicent for a long while. Her mother told me that Millicent, a teenager, recoiled visibly when she first saw him after his stroke and then burst into frantic tears. The change can be very distressing, you know. Odin refused to let her see him again. I'm sure it was to prevent her pain, but she resented the exclusion. Or perhaps she felt guilty—I don't know. So it was only Peter Kugle and Lummie—largely for disciplinary purposes, I should judge, or perhaps matters of business." Why had Millicent twisted that part of the story? I wondered.

"Why is Lummie so afraid of the Eye?" I asked slowly.

"I do not know, Cicely. And if Millicent knows, she has chosen to front for Lummie. Even after he left her, she refused to discuss it."

"Why did Lummie come back here?" I asked.

"Cicely, I don't know. I can't imagine. He must know that he was—is still—disliked. And it's cruel to Millicent. I used to think that he was as dependent on Millicent as she upon him. They often seemed like two drowning people, clutching each other around the neck and going down together. But this summer—lately—I have thought that while she might throw her arms around his neck, he'd be perfectly content to hold his straight to his sides, dragging her down with him, a Mephistopheles incarnate."

Aunt Tattie seemed to have forgotten me. When

she began to speak, I was afraid that I was overhearing thoughts that she had no intention of uttering aloud. "What has Robert done to his life," she asked, so softly I could hardly hear, "that he carries this burden on his back?" I didn't answer. It seemed to me that skeletons had fallen out of closets all over the place. We were both silent, and then Aunt Tattie continued in a stronger voice.

"I simply don't understand the role Olive Plumtree is playing. There has to be some reason for Lummie's return. You see, I have never understood what happened that last day of Odin's life."

"Did Odin see something out of the telescope?" I asked.

"The Eye is not evil in itself," Aunt Tattie said. "But what it sees, or has seen, may well indeed be evil. Millicent has chosen to handle the problem by blinding the Eye. And I have my own guilt to deal with. Out of loyalty to Odin, I should long since have voiced my suspicions. I have always argued that it was not within my power to do so. But I am convinced that the Eye has seen an evil thing, and that Odin died for it."

Then Aunt Tattie looked directly at me. "Cicely," she said, "if you and Geoff have found Peter Kugle's telescope, as I suspect you have, I am fearful that you may be in great danger. Neither of you should be involved in this business."

I didn't know how to answer her. There wasn't any answer. But I had to say something.

"Poor Odin," I said at last.

That night I sat for a little while on my bed, looking back at the Eye, which seemed, as it often did, to search me out, as if it were asking questions, or even challenging me.

I went to sleep at last, but I woke up later with all the same unanswered things on my mind, the same heaviness weighing me down. It was a hot, still night —the ebb tide—and I got up and sat in the Eye looking out. From time to time a ship passed, its running lights gliding across the water. But one little light didn't move. It seemed to blink on and off intermittently. I didn't think there was any pattern to its blinking, rather more than it was rising and falling on the sea swells and perhaps being partially blocked from my view by some object.

Some object like the old buoy midway across the bay, where we had once seen the motor launch with Olive Plumtree aboard. No one went out there, Geoff had said, because of the sea gull stink. But if a boat anchored on the far side of the buoy, you wouldn't be able to see from either shore what went on between the boat and the buoy. Especially at night, unless you had an awfully good telescope.

I had a lot to think about, and I did—a lot of peoples' points of view, including Aunt Tattie's warning. But when I got up and went to the closet for the telescope, it wasn't any of these things or people, not even Geoff, that I was thinking about. It was Odin Fogelsbee.

— Sixteen

I carried the telescope to the window and, working by the glimmer of the nightlight in the hall, screwed it onto the Eye. I could see the buoy as well as if I were sitting alongside in a small boat. The blinking light helped of course, and it did come from a boat—perhaps the same motor launch Olive had used the day the plane went down. I could even make out shadowy figures aboard her, though the buoy was in the way most of the time. I watched for quite a while, but nothing appeared to be happening.

I didn't know what I was looking for, and after a while I decided the whole business was a false alarm. I started to fool around with the telescope, pointing it in this direction and that. All at once the slightest movement on the water caught my attention. I could just make out through the telescope, though the naked eye would never in the world have caught it, the shape of a small unlit dinghy rowing toward the shore. Sometimes I saw it, sometimes I lost it. Then I seemed to catch it in a sort of lurching movement, though that could have been just a trick of the eye. Some time passed while I focused on the little boat, or back to the buoy. I could still see the bobbing light and the shadowy motor launch out there. Then I turned the telescope closer to shore. And froze.

A shiny round black object was floating on top of the water, very near the shore. At first I thought it was a seal, but that was ridiculous: It was too close in. It came nearer, and then as it slowly emerged from the water, I saw to my horror that it was a frogman. He waded silently toward the shore and in a minute was hidden by the seawall where earlier I had been standing and crying. I stopped breathing. I was so shocked that my muscles literally locked me in place. After a short time I caught sight of the rubbery, splay-footed creature again. It returned to the water, slowly submerged, and for a second I saw the round black head and then that was gone, too.

I didn't try to catch the small boat through my telescope again, because I was afraid to move the Eye. I was terrified that the window glass had already caught light from somewhere and showed that it was moving. Right now I needed to watch for something else. Around the corner of the seawall I caught a glimpse of a figure and heard the slightest squelch of wet gravel. I couldn't see, but when I heard a door gently close on the left wing porch, I knew I was right, that Lummie, or else Olive, had been there on the beach under the seawall, that some sort of contact had been made with the frogman, and that the little boat was already on its way back to the buoy. What could I make of this except what Geoff and I had been looking for, what Aunt Tattie probably suspected, and what Millicent, though she tried to suppress it, apparently feared? Some sort of covert action? *Spying?* It was one thing to think it, to play around with the idea. But to *see* it . . . Had the Eye caught Lummie in an act of—treason?

But what if someone else, someone in either of the boats, had caught the Eye in *its* act of spying? Wouldn't Lummie or Olive be contacted at once and warned?

As I began to understand the possibilities, I became more and more terrified.

I hastily unscrewed the telescope and concealed it for the moment in my bedclothes. I had to find a better hiding place for it than the jeans leg and quickly.

I hadn't really done anything about it before—a bad mistake. I had always been uneasy about the closet, but there was so little furniture in that sparse chamber of Odin's, and all of it so plain and purely functional, that I'd never thought anything could have been hidden there. Now I looked around in a panic. I thought of the bathroom, and I rushed in, but everything was exposed, every pipe and piece of plumbing. The construction two-by-fours of the room partition served as shelves, for there was no cabinet over the washbowl, only a mirror. I even checked behind the mirror in my desperation, but there was no opening there. However, the wall made me think.

At this late date it occurred to me that Odin, a neat, shipshape man, would hardly have left an instrument that exquisite just lying around. But any storage place would have to have been within his reach, someplace long and skinny. Why not the wall? There ought to be a space behind the outer wall where it fit in under the eaves. I sat in Odin's rolling chair and began, slowly and with infinite care, though I was shaking with fright, to wheel it around the outer sides of his room. I pushed at the boards within my reach as Odin might have done, the top and bottom of each single piece, desperately hoping that one of them would move.

About halfway up the room, at floor level, a board pushed inward a little. I pushed harder, and the upper section of the board thrust toward me: It was hinged halfway up. Inside was a square shaft, lined with velvet. In relief I rushed to the bed, grabbed the telescope, collasping it hastily, and pushed it into the hidden wall box. But something kept it from sliding in its full length. I hurriedly pulled out the telescope and reached down inside. It was then that I found Odin's log.

The log was handsomely bound in red leather. This didn't surprise me, for although Odin's room was spartan, his telescope was a work of art, and his log would have matched it. The pages were meticulously written, almost as if it had been set in type. Slipped into the flyleaf was a photograph of himself, in dress uniform. It showed, as I expected, a handsome man with correct posture and expression. You would no more have known from the picture what he was thinking or feeling than his crew probably knew as he inspected the ship. Millicent wouldn't have found any softness in that face, I thought. Perhaps that was what she meant by the word "tyrant."

I stowed the telescope safely in its hiding place and then I sat in bed until dawn, reading with my concealed flashlight. I didn't know how much time I had, so I started from the last entry and worked backward.

> 9:32. I hear Robert entering the house. This will be a most serious confrontation.
>
> 8:55. I have sent for Robert L'Hommedieu, intending to confront him with what I fear is an act of treason.
>
> 8:30. Because of my infirmity and my uncertain hold on life, I have been compelled to divulge the details of my discovery to my faithful friend, Peter Kugle. In all honor, it is my duty so to inform Robert. Peter must carry this affair to its proper conclusion in the event of my sudden death.

I sat bolt upright. So Lummie knew that Peter Kugle knew! I hoped Peter Kugle appreciated that act of honor before he was shot. It seemed kind of dumb to me. Women are given to horse sense, which may not be so dramatic as honor, but it has its uses. I didn't have time to ruminate on this.

> 8:15. I will place a call to Peter Kugle. This is the first of a series of acts, which will with-

out doubt sever the relationship between Robert and Millicent, causing infinite pain. I do not doubt that Millicent will be grateful to me in the end. I do not doubt that Robert will suffer shame and ignominy and certain retribution at the hands of the law.

I take this action as a citizen of these United States, and as an officer (ret.) in the U.S. Naval forces, and ultimately for the welfare of my beloved granddaughter.

9/12/56. 4:15 A.M. . . .

I paused at this point, partly to consider what an awful miscalculation Odin had made about Millicent. In the log four hours had elapsed, of what terrible agony, and grief intermingled with rage, I could hardly imagine. I thought of that lonely, crippled man, his family all gone, except Millicent, whom he adored, and of the dreadful decisions he had to make during those hours. I glanced at my watch. It was close to 4:30 and the early summer dawn was breaking. The tide had turned, a strong breeze had dissipated the sticky heat of the night and I was cold, though perhaps not entirely because of the wind.

9/12/56. 4:15 A.M. At 3:10 A.M., unable to sleep, I focused my telescope on the dark bay, intending to watch for the outward passage of the carrier, which I was informed would sail in the early morning hours. I noticed a light by mooring #418 and even though it was partially concealed by the buoy, I detected a motorized launch riding at anchor there. Twenty minutes later my telescope picked up the shadow of a small rowing craft, a dinghy I suspect, nearing a point of shore midway between my home and Kugle's point. None of this, nor the following encounter, would have been visible to the naked eye and I believe it was supposed that a large rock at that point would prevent disclosure of the landing. I saw a figure emerge from the seaward side of the rock, and make contact with the figure in the craft.

At this point, I suspect that certain papers were exchanged. (See entry 4/6/56) I was able to spot the craft later as it returned to Mooring #418 and presumably to the launch waiting there. I am only too aware of the convenience of this contact point, both to a sparsely settled shore and to a near outlet to the sea. In the meantime, in sadness of heart, I watched the figure return to my home, where he has been receiving my hospitality, his own house having burned. I believe that this person, without any doubt whatsoever, was Robert L'Hommedieu.

I turned backwards in the log, glancing hurriedly at entries concerning passing ships and noting in some astonishment that many of them were strong in approval of what he saw.

> 4/6/56. 10:30 A.M. Naval Intelligence, in a most concerned call, informs me that important papers have been reported missing from the agency where Robert has been working. They were making the usual inquiries, mine, under the circumstances, by telephone. I was thankful, considering Robert's troubled career, to report that he is enthusiastic about his work, that I have no indication whatsoever of any involvement with aliens or persons unknown to me. I explained that he had recently announced his engagement to my granddaughter. I assured him that Robert is not in financial need, that he owns a small house next to mine. This seemed to reassure the caller, who explained that the inquiry was merely routine.
>
> It is not just to view a man in light of his youthful follies and Robert is entitled to this much justice.

I thumbed forward again in the log, noting with interest that on June 11, Lummie's house had burned down, and some days later, he had, according to Odin, been able to collect on the insurance. It made me wonder if Lummie were still frantic for money, as Aunt Tattie had said, and if Odin's standards of financial need agreed with his.

The Odin that I was discovering interested me—in fact, the whole business was so storylike that I had almost forgotten my perilous situation. All at once the telephone rang down in the dining room. It was 5:30. I jumped out of bed in alarm, standing barefoot on the rough matting, waiting. I heard Millicent call Lummie to the phone. Had someone seen the Eye move and was this fact being reported back to Lummie? I looked down at the log my in hand and wondered where to put it. I thought that if I shifted the telescope a little, it might slide down the side of the hidden shaft.

I raced to Odin's hiding place and opened it. I pulled out the telescope. Then I heard footsteps on the stairs.

I had just time to drop the log in the velvet shaft, close it and leap to the center of the room, telescope in hand. Lummie stood in the doorway.

— Seventeen

I couldn't believe that Lummie's irresolute face could transform itself in an instant into a thing of such evil intent. Hatred, cunning, malice—all of them were there, and I knew instantly that my life was in danger. I also knew what had so frightened Nate, and I could only imagine with what shock Odin, the man of honor, must have viewed this transformation.

I stepped backwards, but Lummie was upon me at once, his hands on my throat. I felt his thumbs on my windpipe. For a second I thought he was play-acting, as my brother would do in fun, but then I felt an increasing pressure. I thought of Nate. I couldn't believe in that second I would die—it was so completely unexpected, so incongruous. And of course I didn't die. What happened was that a cold voice said, "L'Hommedieu. Leave her alone." And as Lummie's hands left my throat, the voice continued, "They've pulled your chestnuts from the fire once because you were useful to them, but they will not do it a second time." They? The KGB? I stared at Olive Plumtree in horror, weighing the full meaning of the words. I had not heard her footsteps coming upstairs, and in that light, her hollowed face was only a shade less fearful than Lummie's.

I presume we all looked ghoulish, for when Millicent slapped up the stairs, her bedroom slippers half on, half off, her face reflected first astonishment and then a sort of horrified consternation.

"Just exactly what is going on up here?" she asked in a strangled voice, as if she were trying to ward off a blow.

"Lummie was going to kill me," I gasped. Millicent gave me a strange look.

"Nonsense, Cicely," she said.

"He's a spy," I said, beginning to cry. I couldn't help it. "I saw him with the telescope. He was turning something over to the enemy again."

Millicent looked at me in horror, and I rushed on in my recital, gasping out pieces of information between sobs.

"A frogman come up from the sea. Lummie was under the seawall, and he must have given something to the frogman. There was a motor launch waiting out at the buoy, and the frogman went on back to it. Then I heard Lummie come into the house." Lummie lunged toward me, and I heard one of those terrible hisses from Olive. He stopped dead and backed off, though his face still read murder.

I couldn't believe that Millicent could not see Lummie's malice. I thought she would instantly believe my story. Didn't she already suspect Olive and Lummie of this very thing? Instead, she was outraged: I was dead wrong. My tears dried up, and my stomach tightened into a hard knot.

"I never heard anything so ridiculous in my life," she said, her open, honest face reddening in indignation. "What *is* the matter with you, Cicely?"

And then Olive said, in the most scathing tones, "You seem to have a child of fancy up here, Millicent. Fanciful at the least. Perhaps she's even a little bit of a liar."

I couldn't understand why. Olive had been so nice to me the day before—and she'd just saved me from Lummie. I kept looking at her, and after a minute she walked over to the Eye, turning her back on us. That's the ultimate insult of cats. Ours used to do that to us if we went off on a holiday and left her at home alone. As soon as we came home, she'd turn and sit with her back to us.

"I think the spies saw the Eye move," I said, hardly able to utter the words, I was so paralyzed with fear. "I think they telephoned."

"The telephone call," said Olive from the window, and not turning, "was to confirm that Lummie and I are booked on an early plane. We will both be leaving here very soon."

The cruel "both" hit Millicent amidships, and she took a moment to recover. "What, actually, were you doing up here, Lummie?" she asked, her voice shaking a little, but I thought that she was determined to be fair, even to me.

Lummie had said nothing during all this time. He

looked greenish even as the dawn was beginning to grow rosy and warm.

"I've been suspecting that your protegée and Geoff have been spying with that damn telescope," Lummie now said. "Nate kept going on about the Eye seeing again. I knew you'd be disturbed at having the thing in the house, and I came up to get it before I left." He managed to make this sound positively noble. "She wouldn't give it to me," he added.

I still had the telescope clutched in my hand, though had there been a second more with Lummie's thumb on my windpipe, I would have dropped it for sure. "That's *really* a lie!" I shouted, and this time I began to cry in earnest. "You were trying to choke me!"

"Lummie tried to find the telescope earlier," said Olive calmly from the window, "but he was not able to locate it."

"I thought I had been pretty specific about that telescope. I told you and Geoff, both of you, that I didn't want it back in the house. Where did you have it hidden?" Millicent asked.

"In the leg of my jeans," I sobbed. "In the closet." I heard a smothered snort from Olive, but I ignored it. "You wanted me to see what they were up to," I said desperately to Millicent. "You said you thought Olive was a spy."

"Indeed," said Millicent steadily, "I did not."

I was beginning to wonder if I were crazy. I was really desperate. Here I had been half killed and I had uncovered a spy plot, and everyone was calling me a liar. I tried frantically to think back—had Millicent actually said she thought Olive was a spy, or had I just dreamed up the whole thing? Had Geoff and I between us skewed a bunch of perfectly innocent facts?

"I—" I said, and was about to say, "I can prove it," when I shut up. Odin's log lay well-hidden. Lummie couldn't have known about Odin's hiding place or the log, either one. If he had suspected a written record, he would have searched and found the shaft long since. And he must have known that Peter Kugle took the telescope with him after Odin died.

I was up against two or even three powerful enemies—I was beginning to wonder about Millicent—and instinct (or horse sense) told me to keep this last trump card to myself. All three of them were looking at me and waiting for the rest of my sentence.

"I want to go home," I cried.

"And you will," said Millicent carefully. Then she looked straight at Lummie. "You all will," she said, "and what you and Olive intend to do together from now on, I do not care to hear. But you are all going home. I am closing Odin's Eye."

I packed within the hour, raining tears into my suitcase. Regina was going to drive me to the railway station, and we had to hurry. I found Aunt Tattie distraught on the porch, and I sobbed into her arms, "I'm not a liar."

"Oh, Cicely," she said, holding me close. "I am terribly afraid for you." When I looked up at her through my tears, I suddenly realized how very old and trembly she was, how frail, though her plumpness disguised the fact.

"Promise me that you will take this story straight to your parents, Cicely. Will you *promise* me?"

I managed to choke out a yes.

"Oh, Millicent," Aunt Tattie said in despair, "why can't you see? Why *can't* you see?" And she shook me a little. I was afraid she had confused me with Millicent, as Nate had, but she kissed me instead, and said, "I believe you will soon hear from Millicent. She is basically a decent person. But remember, go straight to your parents."

I went home on the train alone, fearful at each station that somehow Lummie would have pursued and caught up with me. I watched the boarding passengers, sick with dread, and if any man in a business suit detached himself from the knots of lumpily dressed humanity at the station, my muscles froze. Each time the train started its jolting departure from the stop, I sank back in my seat in relief.

I hadn't called Geoff to say good-bye; I was ashamed to do so, and in any case, there was neither time nor opportunity, and I was glad of it. I had thought that I would be leaning out the window this very night, my chin in my hands, grieving and listening to the strains of the yacht club band floating across the water. The idea now seemed frivolous and absurd. Geoff, in the face of my present terror, seemed miles away, out of time and place, though I yearned for him just the same, and for the safety and security that he might have given me.

I had said very little to Regina on our hasty trip to the train station. How much she had been told I didn't know, but she muttered, "Such idiocy" as we pulled away from Odin's Eye. It occurred to me that the All-Mothers hadn't kept Asgaard together any better than the All-Fathers. But what did it matter? We were all guilty of seeing with a single eye, even Aunt Tattie, who saw correctly, but was incapable of taking action. Wasn't that a form of blindness? Geoff had tried to understand me, though I'd given him all the wrong signals, but even so, he had some things to learn. Poor Millicent was the blindest of us all. As Mother says, and maybe that was why she had been so worried about sending me to Odin's Eye, "There is none so blind as he who *will not see.*"

I was still looking around for Lummie when I climbed down from the train at our local station. I leaped into a taxi, the first I saw, though I could easily have taken a bus home if I'd dared to wait for it. The taxi cost a mint, and taking one was so contrary to family custom that I had reason to expect repercussions at home. But I was so scared, none of this mattered. I bolted from the cab to the safety of our front door, only to discover that Mother had scarcely noticed the cab and wasn't even aware of my terror. I stood there in the hall, breathing hard and holding out a letter from Millicent, which I assumed told everything. I tried to absorb the fact that Mother was not glad to see me and was making not the slightest effort to conceal her disappointment.

"Your father and I had planned a little trip," she said in a dead voice. "But since you've come home, I guess we'll have to cancel it." She reached for the letter and plunged into it, while I perspired, wondering where to start my story. To my astonishment, her face softened.

"Well, Cicely," she said warmly, "it's nice that you've brought credit on us and yourself, and it *is* too bad that Millicent had to go back to the city." She handed me the letter. There was not one word in it about Lummie, Olive, or spying, not a word about Geoff and the noodle spoon, but a lot of words like *a joy, refreshing, intelligent, and sensible as well.* It was really decent of Millicent.

At the very bottom, in a P.S., she had written, "Caroline, have you noticed that Cicely's knees are a little out of alignment? Shouldn't she be taking some special exercises?"

"What's wrong with your knees, Cicely?" Mother asked absently. My knees? They were knocking together, that's what. But Mother wasn't interested in them. She was really trying to swallow her disappointment.

"I think you and Pop deserve a vacation without kids hanging around your neck," I said slowly. For in spite of my terror, I had begun to think. "I'll go and stay with Winnie. She can always use a hand with Georgie."

Mother soared from despair to joy. "Of course!" She

beamed. "And you can bike over every day and check the house and pick up the mail. I don't like to leave mail in these wretched outside boxes. But how nice of you, Cicely, to be willing to let us go!"

Thus I broke my promise to Aunt Tattie, though I hadn't expected to. I decided instead to take my story to Winnie and John, though I hadn't expected to do that either. But I had one piece of unfinished business.

"Mother," I said, arresting her flight to the telephone and Winnie. "Do you remember mentioning a person named Olive Plumtree who was in your homeroom?"

Mother was all interest.

"Well, she was at Odin's Eye," I said carefully. "She sent her love to you."

"Olive Plumtree!!" cried Mother in delight. "For goodness' sake!"

"Mother, where did she come from, do you know?" I asked.

"They were refugees, from Yugoslavia. Her father was in a prison camp there, a political prisoner. The grandfather got the family out, but the father was sent to Russia and he died there at the hands of the secret police. Olive was very bitter about it. She was a strange girl, but I liked her. What's she like now?"

"I don't know, Mother. I really don't know," I said. And I didn't. I didn't know why she had saved me from Lummie, or been so nice to me out by the seawall. Why had she called me a liar and hurt me so cruelly? I didn't know. Out of all the people at Odin's Eye, in one little conversation, she had made me see where I hadn't been able to see at all. Why had she bothered to do that? I didn't know what to make of this latest information. I wished I didn't admire her. I wished I didn't think she was beautiful. Olive Plumtree was a spy.

— EIGHTEEN

Winnie took one look at me and knew something was wrong. She figured it was boys.

"Well," she asked, "what do you want to do? Take Georgie for a walk in the stroller or go out in the garden and eat worms?"

"I'll take Georgie out in the garden," I said uneasily. "But the real thing is, I have to talk to John the minute he comes home."

"Not boys," commented Winnie. She gave me a shrewd look. "Did a skeleton fall out of a closet perhaps?" she asked.

"Ycs."

"John's coming home early. He's between flights," Winnie said. I drew a slightly longer breath than I had all day. John's off at a moment's notice, at crazy hours —I was really lucky to catch him in.

"Are you safe in the garden?" Winnie asked.

"I don't know," I answered, and she whistled.

"You're safe," John said later, "just so long as that log stays hidden. And as long as Millicent continues to believe that you're a little liar." My story, no details omitted, had had them sitting bolt upright, and when I saw them exchanging glances and heard their awed "wows", I knew I wasn't alone anymore. Sharing the fear didn't lessen the total amount of it, but it did divide it three ways.

"I'll bet Lummie's up in New York right now, charming the life out of Millicent, while he thinks of some way to . . ." John's voice trailed off.

"Do away with me," I said, not cheerfully. "Aunt Tattie thought Millicent would soon figure out the truth. Millicent's not dumb, even if she can't seem to let go of Lummie."

Winnie's comments about Lummie do not bear repeating, but John gave her a sidelong look, and we got back to business.

"I should have brought the log home with me. As proof," I said glumly. "But Millicent helped me pack, and I wasn't really alone. Anyhow, it didn't belong to me."

"Lummie can't possibly know about the log, or he'd have looked for it and destroyed it long ago," John said.

"That's right, I guess," I said slowly. Something was worrying me about this, but I couldn't locate the cause.

"Lummie must have known Peter Kugle took the telescope. He seems to have suspected that Nate had it, anyhow. He wouldn't have been looking for that wall hiding place. But if he got to rooting around in the room now—for some reason—could he find it?"

"No," said Winnie positively. "He couldn't. He couldn't find the telescope when it was hanging inside Cicely's jeans. It's not a characteristic male trait," she pointed out. "Finding things."

"It's hard to locate the right board to push," I said. "The boards are all different widths and lengths."

"Random," said John absently.

"You have to sit in Odin's chair and at just the right height."

"*Olive* might figure it out," Winnie suggested. "If there were some reason for looking." Again I felt that vague uneasiness.

"I don't know if Olive cares that much about Lummie," I said. "What happens to him or anything. She's got him under her thumb—all he does is take orders from her. I think she's just using him. But she might care a lot what happens to me. I can talk." John hmmmed.

"I gather no one knows where you are," he said. "And that's fine. I'll pick up the mail so no one sees you around your place." He thought a lot more.

"I can't fit in this business about the treasure. Regina—was that her name?—sounds pretty convincing about Kidd's travels, and Lummie obviously doesn't believe the treasure bit. What were he and Olive after then? I don't see why they had to get the fisherman out of the way. And if they did vandalize the house . . ."

"Could this Nate have caught whatever the Coast Guard was looking for in his nets?" asked Winnie. "A working model of a communications thing, you said, Cicely. How big would it be? It must have been packed in a box."

I began to get an awful feeling in my stomach. Why hadn't Geoff and I thought of that? The working model. In a box. Lost in the plane crash and caught in the tidal currents. Brought up that morning by Nate, in his fishnet.

"I bet anything Lummie and Olive were planning to get that model to the Russian agents," I said. "Doc said it was on the way to the base where they were working. I'll bet they were going to wait till it got there safely and then steal it and get it to the Russians. They must have known Nate had it. But why would Nate have thought it was the treasure?" No one could answer that one.

"I wonder where he would have hidden it," John said finally. "Cicely, have you any idea?" But I shook my head.

"The other part of the thing I don't understand is Olive Plumtree," John said. "Some of what you've told us doesn't make sense."

"Geoff and I couldn't figure her out," I explained. "The Croatian part. We tried, though."

"This Geoff . . ." said Winnie in a speculative tone.

"I'd better check with the CIA," said John after a lot of thought. He called, and several hours later someone called him back. It was a short conversation.

"They say they have it under control," John reported. He gave me a quizzical look. "You sure walked in on a hot one."

The first letter I got was from Millicent. She said straight out that she had been wrong, that she owed me an apology, and that she had reported the incident to the FBI. She now believed that her grandfather may have seen something of this sort on the day of his death, though she had no proof, and she feared the murder of Peter Kugle would be looked into again. She never wanted to see Lummie again. If I heard any more, I was to let her know. I showed the letter to John, and he frowned.

"Does *anyone* know you're over here with us?" he asked. I shook my head. "You stay put," he ordered. My knees knocked together in answer.

I'd been having bad dreams about Lummie, but now they turned into nightmares. One night I woke up Georgie with my yells. Winnie didn't even scold, though she had to entertain the young man for two hours before he got sleepy again. My terror grew until it filled up the daylight hours as well as the nights.

Three days later John came running in, unusual for him, and hollered for me, at which point *I* came running. Winnie also, Georgie in arms.

"Your next-door neighbor—Edna, is it?—tells me that a tall, rather exotic-looking woman was at your place asking for you. Would that be Olive Plumtree?"

"Yes," I said, growing ice-cold.

"Edna told her you were off with your folks and wouldn't be home until Monday or later." I knew I had just about three days to live.

"Here's another letter for you, Cicely," said John, and he hung around. It was quite a large envelope, about 6 × 8, with a DO NOT BEND written in red, authoritative-looking letters and apparently with something stiff inside to keep it rigid. Its return address was Dr. A. P. Thomas, Thomas Funeral Home, and the address was in New Jersey.

"Is this Thomas your treasure-seeking romantic?" John asked. "What's he writing to you for?" he asked suspiciously.

"He was sort of looking after Nate," I said. "Regina thought he was trying to get the treasure, but she really hated him so much she didn't see all the angles. None of us did," I added hastily. "But I suppose this letter is about Nate."

I shook the envelope, and a letter fell out. I read this first, out loud, since three people (including Georgie in his mother's lap) were patiently waiting.

> Dear Cicely,
>
> Nate died, mercifully I believe, two days ago in the hospital. I visited him there last week. He was very low and did not recognize me, but I am assured that he was treated kindly. Among his effects I found this envelope (enclosed), sealed and addressed to you, and I

> send it on. I am also sending you one of the watercolors from the house. He was fond of you and I believe he would have liked you to have it. The remaining paintings have been sent to the local historical society. They were delighted to have them, for they preserve an era of the Bay which I fear will increasingly be lost.
>
> I am indeed sorry to see Odin's Eye closed up before the season's end and I speculate somewhat on the reason for its untimely end.

"I'll bet," I interjected. "He's probably dying of curiosity."

> I saw to it that Nate had a Christian funeral. A man deserves a fitting end to his life.
>
> Sincerely yours,

and it was signed, Alfred P. Thomas.

Feeling sorry for my remark, because I thought that he'd been decent to Nate after all, I took out the painting. I thought maybe it would be of Odin's Eye, but it was a gentle one of a sunrise over the bridge. I was glad to have it and thought again how nice it was of Doc to send it to me.

"Neat," said Winnie, impressed.

Then I slid out the enclosed envelope, which was addressed to me in Nate's shaky hand. The envelope opened too easily. "Doc must have opened it!" I said in surprise. I looked inside. There were two pencil sketches tucked away in there, on tablet paper, or that's what it looked like. One sketch was the outside of the old windmill, which I recognized right away, and the other one was roughly of the inside.

"What are they?" Winnie asked.

"They're pictures of an old windmill up there," I said slowly. "It's way out in the middle of a field, and no one goes there. Geoff and I did, though."

"Hmm," said Winnie irreverently, but John took the sketches from my hand.

"Look at them carefully, Cicely," he said. "Is there anything different from the way you remember it?"

"Yes," I said at last, my stomach tightening again. "The grain bags were empty when I was there. This shows the one under the bench with something inside it." John sat and thought. Once he looked at his wristwatch, and then he said, "We haven't much time as I figure it."

"For what?" asked Winnie suspiciously.

"For getting up there," John said. "I think your friend Olive opened that inside envelope," he said to me. Winnie grabbed the outside envelope. "I think this was opened, too, with a knife or something, and then relicked."

"Thomas wouldn't have mentioned that the inside envelope was sealed if he planned to open it; or if he did open it, he'd have sealed it up properly," John pointed out. "So if Olive has figured out the picture, and I'll bet a nickel she has, we've got to get up there before she does. She doesn't expect you back before Monday, so I think we have plenty of time. She'll be driving, in any case."

"Well, how are *we* going?" I asked, thinking of the endless train ride.

"We're flying," he said. "I've got a contract tomorrow in Bangor, and we'll go up tonight."

"I ought to let Millicent know," I said.

"When you tell her about that log, she's going to want it anyway," John pointed out. "So we'll have to get into the house, and she has the key. Call her up and ask her to go out to Newark airport just as soon as she can get there. We'll pick her up. I have to make some arrangements," he said. "I've got to have a car ready up there in the boonies, and that's going to be difficult this late."

"Geoff can meet us," I said with conviction.

"Yeah?" said my sister. "I gather he's the subject of some of your woe at least. What's he going to say when you hit him with this?"

"He'll say, 'Well, gee whiz, Cicely,' " I answered. "What I have to listen for is the musical note."

"Cicely, I think you're nuts," Winnie said cheerfully.

"So does Geoff," I responded from the depths of my woe. "And he's right."

"Not by my book," said John in that slow thoughtful way that undoubtedly won Winnie and makes brothers-in-law a national treasure.

I called Geoff first because I knew John and I would be going whether Millicent was available or not.

"Well, gee whiz, Cicely," Geoff shouted in cracked tones, which encompassed at least three octaves, when he heard my voice. It taught me in the future to grieve only when you *know* all is lost.

Then I called Millicent. She was absolutely stunned when I told her about the wall hiding place and the log. "He wouldn't let me in his room," she said. "I had no idea . . . oh, dear God!" she exclaimed in distress. "I hope *Lummie* . . . Cicely, I'll leave here this minute, and I'll be waiting for you at the airport."

"John," said Winnie in a commanding voice. "I want you to be careful! You too, Cicely," she mentioned as an afterthought.

"Adventure is the spice of life," John said kissing her. "I'll get Nancy Drew here back to you by tomorrow." Winnie laughed, but I thought she hung onto him a little longer than she usually did when he left, and I didn't feel like laughing at all.

— NINETEEN

"Oh, if Mother could see me now!" I thought as we bounced along in John's little plane. And then I put the thought from my mind, for although parents add a continuo (I am speaking musically) of anxiety to an adventure of this kind, they rarely contribute to the outcome, which is why, in books, they are usually off on vacation, or in the hospital, or in stark cases, dead. I had plenty at hand to occupy me anyhow without agonizing over parental nerves.

We picked up Millicent, who looked terrible but determined. In her case there was plenty of opportunity for martyrdom, considering what a rat Lummie had turned out to be, but Millicent hasn't the build of a martyr. Right then she looked more like a general in the Salvation Army.

Geoff may have had a more elegant greeting in mind than what transpired at the airport, but John, still on the run, said, "Hurry it up, kid," and we piled into Geoff's car, overnight bags in hand, without salutation. In fact, Geoff, in his haste, shot the car straight up to the very heavens from which we had just descended and killed the motor. John's look of patient exasperation didn't bode well for Georgie in his teens, I thought.

It was about 9:30 P.M., already dark enough for headlights. We had to go a distance of several miles, and John sat up in front with Geoff looking very intently at cars as they passed and checking the side mirror. Several times he turned and looked out the back window. Millicent and I, in the rear, said absolutely nothing. She sat up perfectly straight, looking composed, but I wouldn't have given a plugged nickel for the state of her stomach. The country roads, which looked so wild-rosy in the daytime, now seemed threatening, and I kept expecting to see cars appearing out of the overgrown and hidden driveways.

"Speed it up," said John. "We could do with a cop." There weren't any—there never are when you need them—and pretty soon we turned into the little-used road that leads to the mill.

"Turn off your lights," said John. And then, with a little hesitation, "Mind if I take the wheel? *Don't slam your door!*" They exchanged places very quietly, and John, who must have had good night vision from flying in darkness, drove carefully up the lane.

"Here," said Geoff in a low voice. "We have to walk." John backed the car into a little stub of road and turned it, heading out.

"Stay together," John said. "*Don't slam the doors!*" although no one was going to. On the edge of the open field John looked around—we all did—and then we started for the mill. You could see it sort of huddled down in the field, very black against a little lighter sky. We really tore across that open field.

The door was unlocked, and with the help of John's flashlight, which he masked with his hand, I led the way to the bench where the grain bags were. They were still there all right, but one of them was heavy when I tried to pull it out. In a minute we had the box, and John took just time enough to flick his flashlight over the square block letters on the outside.

PROJECT KIDD

"Poor Nate," murmured Millicent. "No wonder he was confused."

"Why is it called Kidd? That's crazy," Geoff observed.

"I'm sure Lummie named it," Millicent said. "The model was his project. It was certainly part of the plot to come to Odin's Eye with Olive this summer in order to make their contacts. It's just like him to come up with a bizarre name like that."

"I guess he didn't expect to get mixed up with Nate and old Doc Thomas," I commented.

"Just his luck," said Millicent.

Tough, I thought.

"On the double," said John, coming back to business. He took the box, and we streaked across the field, back to the car. Oddly enough I didn't feel one bit safer inside it than I had out in the black, exposed field. John simply got in behind the wheel, and then he said in that slow voice, "No one knows me, so I'm okay, but you three are going to have to sit on the floor. Geoff, I'll tell you when to look out so you can give directions to Odin's Eye." Millicent and I crouched down on the floor of the backseat, Kidd's treasure between us, and nothing else but silence. It takes forever to go somewhere when you can't see and everything is deathly still.

"You go down this back road to the end," Geoff said softly. "You make one lefthand turn. You can turn around at the end." John must have turned out his lights again, because Geoff said uneasily, "It's pretty dark, and the road's not that good."

"Can you drive into the yard?" John asked after a lot of jolting.

"Not really," said Geoff. "There's no place to turn." More jolting as John swung the car around, facing out again.

"Stay together," he whispered. "I'll carry the box. Let's make it snappy." We got out, all four of us, and running through the dark garden, headed for the kitchen door. Millicent hurriedly unlocked the rusty, old-fashioned lock.

"Lock us in," said John, and Millicent turned the key on the inside and put it in her handbag.

Talk about haunted houses! In the wintertime the windows were boarded up, but the caretaker hadn't had time to do it, so the black glass stared at us as we tiptoed toward the stairs. The living room, usually so mellow at night in the lamplight, was a chamber of horrors—even the furniture seemed to watch us, and the outside chairs piled up in front of the porch door looked like a ghastly shipwreck in the glimmer of the bay lights.

We ran upstairs, making what seemed a thunderous noise. The Eye focused on us with that curiously alive look that it had when the bay lighted it from behind. It stopped me dead in my tracks.

"The Eye's open!" Millicent hissed. "I left it closed!" She rushed to the dresser and flung open a drawer. "The telescope's gone! Lummie *has* been here!" she cried. "I knew it!" She dropped her handbag on one of the chairs and began opening all the drawers, one after another. I must say that even John looked green in what little light we had from the outside. He kept glancing at the unblinking, terrible Eye.

"Here's the telescope," whispered Geoff. He pulled it out from under the pillow of the stripped-down cot.

"See if he found the log, Cicely." John shook my arm. "Hurry *up!*"

I rushed to the wall shaft and reached in. I thought my fingers would grasp only emptiness, but the log was exactly where I'd dropped it. Millicent didn't say a word as I handed the little notebook to her.

Something forced all four of us at once to look back at the Eye, the way you look over your shoulder when you sense something behind you, or think someone is watching you. Something besides the Eye, though that was awful enough. I looked down at the water.

"John!" I cried, sick with terror. The shiny round head, the frogman, was coming out of the water, right in front of the cottage. Even as John spotted it, the shoulders followed.

We made for the stairs, all four of us clattering down helter-skelter, and we dashed through the other rooms to the kitchen.

"Oh! My bag! I left it upstairs!" Millicent cried in despair. "The key's in it."

"Out the hurricane window!" ordered Geoff, flinging it open, and we scrambled out, then ran pell-mell back through the garden to the car.

As we burst from the garden, we found the car, doors open, waiting for us, and beside it, Olive Plumtree. The inside car light glinted off her revolver.

"Get in," she said. "Quickly." And to John, "You in front, Mr. Rapp. You'll be driving. I'll take Kidd's treasure, thank you," she continued quietly. "And if that's the log Lummie has been looking for, I'll have that too, Millicent."

— TWENTY

When Winnie gives John too many orders, there's usually a big argument, but this time he didn't say a word. He just looked respectfully at the revolver and slid in the front seat. "Quickly," repeated Olive, and the three of us got in in a hurry. If it came to the frogman rising from the sea or Olive Plumtree, I'd take my chances on Olive, though it was a Hobson's choice at best. What with John at risk in the front seat, all of us captive, Project Kidd in the hands of the enemy, there wasn't much room for optimism.

"Drive back to the windmill," said Olive. If it had been a TV show, the cops would have added, "and no funny stuff," but Olive didn't need to put any embellishment on her statement. She sat there, really beautiful in the dashboard lights, but I couldn't have been more scared if a panther were crouched in the front seat. John drove, and the three of us sat in back like rounded-up truants from school, not moving a muscle. Olive didn't even bother to look at us.

We marched back across the field, escorted by Olive, and were met by two stern-looking men at the door.

They tied our hands and feet. I was not cheered to see that they had the materials readily available and did the job with professional efficiency. One of them spoke to Olive in a low voice, and she answered so softly that I couldn't tell whether they were speaking English or Russian. It was at that point that they gagged us. All three worked at top speed, but in the end they propped us up rather comfortably against adjoining walls, which was at least halfway decent of them. Olive hesitated in the doorway and looked down at Millicent, who was shaking all over. One of the men had made John take off his aviator's jacket before they tied him up, and Olive went over and draped this around Millicent's shoulders. Before they locked the door, they put a flash-light on the millstone in the center and tied a handker-chief over the end of it. This gave a dim light, enough so we could at least see each other. I thought both these gestures were pretty humane for spies. It made me think all over again about cats who play with their captured mice and then, calmly finish them off.

I looked across the corner of the room to Geoff. His long legs stuck straight out, and he was doing all kinds of eyebrow raising and shoulder shrugging. Communi-cation under conditions like these is limited, so after I had done the same, I glanced at Millicent. She is quite devout in her religion, so when I saw her closed eyes I thought she might be engaged in some sort of peti-tion, but then I saw tears roll down her cheeks. I was about to look hastily away when she opened her eyes and I saw to my astonishment that she was having a fit of temper. She was absolutely boiling over. Her eyes looked exactly like Georgie's when Winnie has taken away his bottle.

And then I discovered a remarkable thing. John, all six feet four inches of him, was sprawled out on the floor beside me, and his chest was rising and falling in a slow rhythm as if he were sound asleep. If he hadn't been gagged, I wouldn't have been surprised at all to hear him snore.

No one falls asleep who's just been captured by Russian spies. I gazed at him in consternation. He then opened one eye and gave me a long, lascivious wink. I was so shocked that I sat straight up. Old Doc Thomas, maybe, a wink like that. But *John . . .?*

I stared at him in absolute horror, and he winked again, another slow, deliberate, sultry, heavy-lidded wink.

I glanced at Geoff. His eyelashes were arching, and he lifted both feet off the floor and banged them down. He must also have been watching John. I set in to think —hard.

How come John, who was scared stiff of Olive in the car, was all of a sudden so all-fired relaxed? He wasn't afraid of her anymore. Why not?

Geoff and I had always just *assumed* that Olive was a spy, a Russian agent. *But what if she wasn't?* I started thinking all over again about Olive Plumtree, but this time I thought in the opposite direction.

Suppose: Olive is an expert in electronic surveillance. We know this. The CIA is trying to find the source of a leak in satellite communications. Perhaps Olive Plumtree is known to them because of her inquiries about her father in Russia. She speaks Croatian and probably Russian. So they approach her. Lummie could have been passing material to the enemy for a long time. Though probably, after Odin caught him, he stopped for awhile. But finally he needed more money. . . . Anyway, how does Olive find Lummie?

She can try to find the agency spy, probably an American. Or a Russian acting as an American.

OR

Here I sat up, as much as I could, anyhow, the light having dawned. I saw Geoff wigwagging eyebrows, and I wigwagged back, hoping my eyes spelled *Eureka,* but doubting it.

OR (to continue)

The American Science Press!

The Russians are known to keep track of scientific and technical developments in America. So Olive gets their attention through a book, published by the American Science Press. The Russians, spotting her Yugoslavian name, contact her, feel her out. She goes to Russia and Yugoslavia. Which is where Mayne Cooper saw her. She locates Robert L'Hommedieu and his agency through the Russian spy system. She finds out that he has access to crucial materials that the

Russians want. They work with him, even though he is not trusted by the KGB because of his mishandling of the Kugle affair. The KGB, needing more materials, must have decided to alibi him out of suspicion in the Kugle murder, which he committed all right, and . . .

Did Lummie also kill Odin by trying to choke him? Perhaps, infuriated, or shocked, Odin was catapulted into his fatal stroke. No wonder Lummie broke the engagement! How could you marry someone when you knew you'd murdered her grandfather, or at least caused his death? He must have been terribly afraid that Millicent would somehow find out about him. And yet he had kept some contact with her over the years to make sure no suspicions arose.

I thought about fear, the terror I'd lived in for almost a week, the dread of each face on the train, each telephone call at Winnie's and I thought of the *twenty-five years* of fear that Lummie would have lived with. No wonder his face was so haunted, so malevolent.

But now I got to thinking about the log. Did Lummie suspect that Odin had kept a log? Did he hunt for it at the time of the murder? I thought the answer to both these questions was no. But then why was he *recently* hunting for it, and how did Olive know about the log? Again I had the uneasy feeling that I got whenever I thought about the log. Had I given myself away at some point? I frowned, I guess, because Geoff pounded with his feet a second time and signaled all kinds of questions and alarms. I signaled in return, "Hang in there," and continued to think.

I couldn't answer the above questions, so back I went to Olive. The American agents didn't have to fool around with Lummie; they now knew all the facts about his spying. So the CIA must be using him, with Olive's help, to go after bigger game. Perhaps one of the KGB's top agents. Or a whole bunch of them at once.

If my hunch about the American Science Press was correct, the CIA has been planning a spy bust for several years. I began to wonder if maybe this whole thing was a war of secret agents, theirs and ours. And Olive taking revenge . . .

At any rate, Olive obviously contacted Lummie. She and Lummie "decided" to make their contacts at Odin's Eye, because of the easy access to the sea, as Odin's log had pointed out. After all, no hint of discovery had come to light in all of those years, and Lummie must have thought it safe enough to reuse the territory. Olive "helped" Lummie plot to send the working model, PROJECT KIDD, to the KGB.

The plane went down and spoiled their plans. I didn't know how Olive or the CIA had planned to retrieve the model before it got to the Russians, but I thought the plane going down had been an unexpected development. After that, both Lummie and Olive for separate reasons, would have been watching to make sure, if the model were found, it didn't get into the wrong hands.

When Nate found "Kidd's treasure" and hid it, they both had to go into action, Olive secretly from Lummie. Hence the vandalism, etc., etc. In the meantime, other important documents were "leaked" while Olive made plans for the big haul. Probably everything had come to a head because she had discovered where the "treasure" was hidden.

But who came along and bollixed up the whole scene?

Cicely Barrows, detective. And Geoff, aiding and abetting in ferreting out secret facts, spying with the telescope, and in the end, both of them showing up complete with brother-in-law and Millicent in tow, making off with the treasure, and turning up at Odin's Eye right in the middle of the whole spy bust. *If* I was right, that is.

Geoff was about to explode, since emotions, as I have already pointed out, cavort across my face like a TV screen, and even when I'm gagged anyone can see that things of moment are happening. I looked at John. He winked again, but this time his eyes were laughing.

How come John knew just who to call up the other night? John and his airplane VIPs. He must have recognized one of the guys who tied him up. Probably he flew him to Newport or somewhere in his plane.

We sat there for two hours, and that's a long time when you're gagged and choking and sitting tied up on a hard floor. But it must have been worse for Millicent and Geoff. At least I had some hope.

Geoff and I had both given up signaling, the way you do when you're outside a train waiting for it to pull out and you've already said goodbye to your relative inside, but the train refuses to leave. You use body language for awhile, and then you just stay there dolefully for hours looking at each other through the glass.

Finally we all heard a car and returning footsteps. We sat up straighter and then the door opened and Olive came in. She looked old and tired, and she went right to Millicent, untied her, and took her outside. Then the two men came in and untied John.

"Sorry," one of them said.

"Get your man?" John asked, standing up and stretching to about nine feet five.

"The lot," he said. "But it was touch and go. L'Hommedieu was killed. Olive's breaking the news to Miss Fogelsbee."

The other man started on Geoff. "What's going on?" Geoff demanded as soon as his gag was removed.

"You folks walked in on a little do we've planned for six or seven years, that's all. Uninvited guests. Sorry to treat you so impolitely, but we didn't have much choice. For one thing, when Olive's in her Russian role, as she was tonight, you don't fool around with her or you're apt to get shot. She plays it absolutely straight. You were awfully close to being caught by one of the Russian agents, and we didn't want you to know *anything.* We wanted you to look pretty damn scared in case they did find you. We didn't count on Mr. Rapp's showing up, I can tell you: That's why you were all gagged. You can blame him." Geoff just stood there looking at the CIA man and blinking like a barn owl.

Olive came back in and stooped down beside me. The minute she got the gag off, I asked her how come Lummie knew about the log.

"The one little word, '*again*'. That was a mistake. Think back to the scene in Odin's room." She laughed, throwing back her head and chuckling in her secret, amused way. "I'll put you on the CIA waiting list," she said. "You're a natural." We both stood up, me stiffly.

"Millicent's in the car," she said, handing the keys, not to John, but to Geoff. "She'll be feeling bad, but there wasn't much ahead for L'Hommedieu." Olive looked down at me and tilted up my chin with one finger. "Well, Cicely, till we meet," she said, and laughed again, deep in her throat. Then she was gone, followed by the other two. Geoff put his hands on my shoulders.

"Come on, Cicely," he said. "Who is she?"

"She's a double agent," I answered. "How could we have been so blind?"

Geoff continued to look down at me, and I began to feel like a snowman in spring. I saw John glance at us and tactfully slip out the door.

Geoff put his arms tight around me and gave me a great masterful kiss. A hot knife started at the top of me and cut me in half. Then Geoff suddenly sprang away from me, leaping backwards.

"Well, gee whiz, Cicely," he complained.

And then we both laughed. We sat down close together on the old bench, and Geoff took my hand.

"I think Millicent ought to go straight back to Odin's Eye," I said. "She ought to knock out the Eye and put in a double window."

Geoff didn't answer for a minute.

"You say the craziest things, Cicely," he said at last.